NAPOLEON & JOSEPHINE

GERALD AND LORETTA HAUSMAN

ISBN: 0-439-56890-0

Length:
288pp

Retail Price:
$16.95 US
$22.99 CAN

Ages:
10 & up

LC: 2003020257

Scheduled Pub. Date:
October 2004

Trim:
5 1/2" x 8 1/4"

Classification:
Historical Fiction

Grades:
Sixth grade & up

ORCHARD BOOKS
An Imprint of Scholastic Inc.
557 Broadway, New York, NY 10012

The Sword &
the Hummingbird

Napoleon &

the Sword

Gerald &

Josephine

& the Hummingbird

Loretta Hausman

ORCHARD BOOKS
AN IMPRINT OF SCHOLASTIC INC.
NEW YORK

LIBRARY OF CONGRESS CATALOGING-IN-PUBLICATION DATA
Hausman, Gerald; Hausman, Loretta.
Napoleon and Josephine: the sword and the hummingbird /
by Gerald & Loretta Hausman   p.   cm.
Summary: From her childhood in Martinique, Josephine knew that she would someday be "more than a queen," and she eventually fulfills her destiny at the side of Napoleon Bonaparte as Empress of the French.
ISBN 0-439-56890-0
[1. Josephine, Empress, consort of Napoleon I, Emperor of the French, 1763–1814 — Juvenile fiction. 2. Napoleon I, Emperor of the French, 1769–1821 —Juvenile fiction. 3. Josephine, Empress, consort of Napoleon I, Emperor of the French, 1763–1814 — Fiction. 4. Napoleon I, Emperor of the French, 1769–1821 —Fiction. 5. Kings, queens, rulers, etc. — Fiction. 6. France — History — Consulate and empire, 1799–1815—Fiction.] I. Title.
PZ7.H2883 Nap 2004   [Fic] — 22   2003020257
10 9 8 7 6 5 4 3 2 1   04 05 06 07 08

Printed in the U.S.A.
Reinforced Binding for Library Use
First edition, October 2004

The text was set in 22-point Goudy. The display type was set in P22 Cezanne Regular and Bodoni Sev Swash ITC Bold Italic.

Book design by Marijka Kostiw

Some people might wonder why our cultural obsession with Napoleon and Josephine has led to thousands of biographies. Have we not heard their story often enough? Why is their personal life so interesting to readers of books and viewers of films almost two hundred years after their death? What is the seemingly permanent attachment that we hold for these two people?

Napoleon and Josephine seem more from our time than theirs. They were mythmakers. They created themselves out of their own fancy. Although her name was Rose, he called her Josephine because it sounded aristocratic; she called him Bonaparte, as if he were just another general.

Josephine was an island girl from Martinique in the French colonies. Napoleon was a Corsican-born, island-bred Italian, who could claim to be French only because France captured the island the year he was born.

Neither Napoleon nor Josephine had any ties to the

kind of royalty they aspired to emulate and become. They were survivors, each of them, and they lived buoyantly and desperately in a world that was constantly threatening to sink beneath them.

The history that brought Napoleon and Josephine together was violent and cruel. The French Revolution was founded on the same principles as the American Revolution — restoring the common man to power — but to achieve that, the rich, the royals, and the monarchs had to tumble. Thus one of the worst bloodbaths in human history ensued.

As a young and talented general, Napoleon saw the need for a democratic France. However, his method of achieving equality was through the sights of his gun. Napoleon, the skilled cannoneer, was a master of might who dominated Europe in the postrevolutionary period by the force of his munitions as well as the brilliance of his strategies. He moved his men fast and hard and left his enemies no quarter in which to hide or retreat.

Napoleon's credo was the Empire, and he strove to

achieve dominance by overpowering Austria, Italy, Spain, Prussia, Russia, and Egypt — in a lightninglike fashion. In the end, though, Napoleon understood that his great battles could be forgotten, but that his Civil Code, the code of municipal law, would be around forever. In many countries, it still exists exactly as he wrote it because it is both universal and practical.

Josephine, no less than Napoleon, changed the world in which she lived as well. She collected art treasures and left behind a legacy of paintings and sculptures that still draws visitors from all over the globe. Josephine possessed a scientist's curiosity and a collector's acquisitiveness. Her waterfalls, streams, ponds, lakes, terraces, and grottoes are a landscaper's dream. On islands, pale willows and pink rhododendrons grow side by side. Her home, Malmaison, is itself a work of art.

Yet it is not what Napoleon and Josephine left behind but rather what they did not that still haunts us. Their relationship, an intriguing fog of gossip and romance, compels renewed interest in this famous couple. The way they lived and loved — this, more than anything — holds our fascination.

Napoleon and Josephine fought bravely for what was theirs — a not-too-brief, always impulsive, ever passionate, unusually destructive, and sometimes insane love affair. And with an endless backdrop of bloodshed, battlefields, sewers, and salons, these two traipsed about like players in their own private drama. Today, most of what we know of them is based upon what other people have said. No doubt they knew that one day we would be sifting through the ashes, looking for something that is not there.

*Note to the reader:
Some books about Napoleon and Josephine use French accents on their names. We have chosen not to do this to make the text more accessible to English-speaking readers.

The Hummingbird

One

Martinique, 1777

Rose Tascher de La Pagerie spent her fourteenth birthday on the second floor of her family's sugar mill on the French West Indian island of Martinique. Through the open shutters of the verandah she saw the turquoise sea crawling in slow, sluggish swells up the dark volcanic beach. But most of all Rose's gaze was met by the gardens of green, the tropical fruit trees, the giant ferns, the far-off fretwork of forest and farm. Trois-Ilets was a place of dark emerald beauty, and Rose loved it as one loves something that cannot love back. But that did not matter — not to her, anyway. For she was a hummingbird darting among the flowers.

Now she looked beyond the buildings and barns to the rush-roofed slave quarters. She saw the fields where her father's red cattle grazed all the way to the great blue forest, a labyrinth of creepers and trees that rose steeply from the green hollow of La Pagerie.

Below the house lay the gray ruins of the fallen plantation building where the family had lived until the hurricane of 1776 forced them to move into the stone sugar mill. Off to the east the waters of the river glimmered with the twilight shapes of white geese that had settled along the riverbank for the night. The first fireflies were making their long, lazy, blinking loops in the soft velvet air. The tree frogs were singing and darkness crept, little by little, between the trees and filled the spaces between them with ink.

Rose had spent the day indoors because of a gentle, persistent rain that turned the lawns into sponge. Now the rain had stopped, and she ached to go outside under the dripping breadfruit trees. She'd promised to walk along the riverbank with her favorite cousin, Aimée.

"Can I go, Maman?" Rose pleaded. "For just a little while? I'll be back before the lighting of the candles."

Madame de Tascher smiled indulgently. "The candles are being lighted *now*," she said.

Rose pouted. "I promised Aimée. It's my special day, Maman."

Claire de Tascher said, "Of course it is, *ma chérie*. That's why I want you here with us. Your nurse, Gertrude, has made the most beautiful cake from the finest cocoa of the estate, and your sisters are beside themselves with excitement."

Madame de Tascher sighed, then relented. "Go ahead, find Aimée, and fly home swiftly."

Like an arrow shot from a bowstring, Rose was gone down the wrought-iron stairs, which rang under her bare feet. Down she went, *cling-clang-clung*. She darted through the hibiscus arbor. A slight brush of her shoulder brought a cascade of cold tickly waterdrops onto her bare neck. Where the red dirt road made a bend, Rose's cousin Aimée waited. Squealing when they saw each other, the two girls hugged and laughed in the shadowy light.

Some steps hence, sitting underneath a tamarind tree, was the aged sorceress, Eliama. Rose's mother called her Sybil because, like the Greek goddess, she had the ability to see into the future. Rose and Aimée sat on the grass next to old Sybil, and asked to have their fortunes told.

For a long time the turbaned old woman gazed deeply into the outstretched palms of the two girls. As she did so the darkness closed softly about them like a dark silk shawl. Fireflies made dancing loops over their heads. Down the road, the candles of Trois-Ilets twinkled on the verandah of the old sugar mill. Already it was time to go home. And already Rose felt anxious.

After the longest time, the old woman mumbled the names of the saints — some in French and some in Dahomey. Then she looked into Rose's eyes and said, "You will be unhappily married and widowed."

"Is that all?" Rose looked doubtfully at Aimée.

Eliama said, "You will be more than a queen."

Rose glanced at Aimée again, her eyes excited.

"What will I be, then?" Aimée asked.

"You," said Eliama, her voice lowering, "will be something less. . . ."

Aimée's face fell. Eliama bent her watchful eyes close to Aimée's outstretched hand, peering at the wrinkles and lines.

". . . and something more!" she said grinning. "Now both of you, run along home. Mind your feet — serpents are out!"

"More than a queen!" Rose exclaimed as the girls ran on the wet clay road, leaping over every stick and root in their path.

"Something *less*, something *more* . . . heavens, what can that be?" Aimée wondered aloud.

The iron stairs rang on their arrival. The candled cake was set out, alight, on the table as they rushed onto the verandah.

Two

Martinique, 1777–1778

Joseph de Tascher rubbed his tired eyes. It was very late and he was worn out from the long day. However, there was a sailing ship leaving for France early in the morning, and his letter had to go with it. To him, and to his family, this letter was a matter of life and death.

"I am," he wrote, "a wealthy man — not in funds but in daughters, the greatest richness a man could ever want, or have."

He raised his goose-quill pen and used the feather end to brush away a moth. The house was still but for the piping of tree frogs outside. Joseph glanced again at his sister's letter from Paris, to which he was writing his response. His good fortune was having a sister, Rose's aunt Edmée, who was the godmother of Vicomte

Alexandre de Beauharnais. Not only was this splendid seventeen-year-old handsome and rich and titled, but he was also seeking a wife!

Moreover, Alexandre had spent his first seven years in Martinique. And Edmée was herself engaged to Alexandre's father. All of this spoke well for a family-arranged marriage for one of his daughters. The question was, which one?

Joseph glanced at the letter from Edmée. The description of Alexandre was too good to be true. "Attractive of both face and form . . . he has both wit and talent . . . all the good qualities of heart and soul are united in his character. . . . He is loved by all who know him."

Holding his sister's letter closer to the slender flame, Joseph's eye fastened on the most engaging line of all. This was the one that said no dowry was required, just a suitable bride. Too, another sentence said that "as soon as Alexandre is married, he shall receive his inheritance."

Joseph sighed and put down his quill. He looked at his writing table. The children's fans, cast aside before they went to bed, lay amidst a treasure of freshly gathered fruit — mangoes, pawpaws, naseberries, tamarinds, and tiny finger bananas.

"All these she must leave behind," he said to himself. Joseph sighed again. "Yet all of this *I* would gladly give up for one look at the thousand windows of gold in the great palace of Versailles."

Smiling, he selected a ripe little rose-colored banana, which he peeled and ate in one bite.

"Maybe not," he chuckled as he licked his fingers and blew out the candle.

"What did your letter say, *mon chéri?*" asked Claire de Tascher the next morning after the children had gone on their walk to La Pagerie River with Euphémie, known as Mimi. She was a household helper, but most of all Rose's constant companion. They'd been friends since birth.

"Well," Joseph replied, "I explained to Edmée that all three daughters are . . . ," he searched for the right word, "a possibility."

Claire poured Joseph's coffee from a swan-necked pewter urn. From silver to pewter, they were a family who refused to be down on their luck, though that was clearly the case.

Claire frowned. "You didn't say anything about our eldest and most desirable — the most obvious choice?"

"You mean our little Rose?"

Joseph set down his coffee cup. "Alexandre's father has already expressed a preference, I'm afraid. He wants to find a suitable bride."

"Suitable . . . in temperament, or in looks?"

Joseph took another sip of coffee.

"Neither one. Alexandre wants a bride who is not so close to him in age. Rose is fifteen, he is seventeen. So Catherine — being thirteen — is a better choice for him. Manette is too young — a child still. That's what I said in my letter, which, if the courier went directly to the wharf, is already at sea. So, in a few short months we shall have our answer."

More than three months later, the letter finally came. It took a long time for mail to cross the Atlantic. As Joseph had guessed, Catherine was Alexandre's choice. Yet when he saw her name, so plain, so boldly scripted, he burst into tears. For in the time that had passed between his letter leaving Martinique and Alexandre's reply from Paris, a terrible tragedy had befallen the family. Catherine, his beloved second-born, had caught a fever and died. This happened often in the tropics, and the once-lovely girl was already in her grave.

In spite of this crushing sorrow, Joseph still had to select a bride for Alexandre. Now, more than ever, it was a financial necessity. With one daughter gone, he had that much less to bank on. The horrible truth was that they were desperately poor, and their daughters' marriages were a richer and readier crop than the cane that grew in their fields.

Alexandre insisted on a de Tascher bride, and as it stood, the most likely bride-to-be was still Rose. But the marquis, Alexandre's father, had been adamant about the closeness of her age and his son's. This was a social indiscretion that he stubbornly opposed.

Manette, the youngest daughter, was therefore next in line. But at eleven and a half, she was far too young.

What was Joseph to do? Should he wait until Manette was of a marriageable age?

After talking it over with Claire, Joseph decided to suggest Rose one last time. Picking up his goose quill, he wrote of her beauty and manner and made her less desirable than irresistible. He poeticized her virtue, sweetness, and grace in such an exotic and flowery way that he couldn't resist calling her his "little hummingbird of the Indies."

Yes, he thought, *that will do it.*

And so, another three months went by slowly until at last the long-awaited letter from Edmée came.

That day Rose was swinging in a hammock with

Manette. It was too hot to go out into the sun. Rose had caught a bright green lizard, and was telling it a story about Paris in the spring. In Martinique, it was also spring. But in the West Indies no one noticed the seasons as much because the flowers were always blooming and the sun was always shining.

"You would have need of boots," Rose explained to the lizard. "The streets are muddy and dirty in Paris this time of year."

She put the green lizard next to her ear.

"What is that you say? You don't wish to wear boots? You want to run about naked in the snow?"

Claire de Tascher came onto the porch. "Aunt Edmée's letter's come," she said all out of breath. The two sisters sat up straight in their hammock.

"Who longs to go to Paris?" Claire asked.

Manette nodded, made a frown, shook her head. Glancing at Rose's pet lizard, she replied, "There aren't any pretty lizards in Paris, are there, Maman?"

"There are gorgeous ladies and handsome gentlemen,"

Rose told her younger sister. Then, handing the lizard to Manette, Rose queried, "Am I to pack, Maman?"

Claire put her hand to her mouth. "You already *know?*"

And Rose answered, "Don't you remember when Eliama read my palm?"

Three

Brest & Paris, France
1779

The moment Rose set foot in France, she felt strange, and frightened. Even though her father and Mimi were with her and made her feel less homesick, Rose fought with many hidden fears. *Was she good enough to be the future wife of a vicomte? Would he really love her? Was she pretty enough? Were her clothes suitable?*

The day Alexandre came to the inn where Rose and her father were staying, Rose trembled all over. A black carriage drawn by a matched pair of flashy sorrels clattered into the courtyard. The coach door opened. Out stepped a tall, fair-haired soldier. He wore a white uniform with silver trim. In the bright sun of Brest, he looked mature and self-assured.

Rose's heart jumped. Alexandre smiled at her, but only faintly. She looked at him in swift, small, hungry glances, so that he wouldn't see her staring. He had straight teeth, fine hair, and soft azure eyes. The black sword at his side made Rose think of a picture she'd seen in a book. Alexandre was everything she had imagined — and more. Yet this only caused her to feel less certain of herself. What had *she* to offer *him*? Was he too grand a prospect for her?

One fleeting smile from him brought back her confidence.

I am talented, she thought. *I can play the guitar. I can dance — not well but passably. In Fort-Royal I whirled with the best of them. My singing voice is good, too. So is my speaking voice. And I've got a fine little bow of a smile — everyone at Trois-Ilets says so — but I mustn't open my mouth too wide because if I do he'll see that some of my teeth are not as perfect as his. . . . If only I hadn't eaten so much sugarcane when I was little.* These sudden eddies and currents swept through Rose's mind as she smiled — but not too widely — for Alexandre.

After the briefest introduction and the shortest conversation ever, Alexandre excused himself with an abrupt rudeness that, once again, caused her to lose her footing. He had pressing duties to perform, he said, and as quickly as he'd come, Rose's future husband went away.

In his father's coach, Alexandre confided to the marquis, "Rose is not the prize she was purported to be — far from it."

The marquis gave his son an irritable glance.

Alexandre ignored it and went on, "It's not your intention to have me marry this provincial girl, is it? *Mon dieu, mon père*, the little beast's frightened out of her wits just looking at me! How could I possibly fall so low as to marry her?"

The marquis clamped his lips and said nothing. He knew that if Alexandre didn't seal the bond of marriage, the young man wouldn't receive his mother's inheritance. That was the law: An underage man couldn't come into his fortune without a wife. As far as the marquis was concerned, the match was a business deal. If French law had demanded his son marry a heifer, he would have seen it done with the same alacrity.

Finally he said, "I'm afraid you're going to have to bear with your bride-to-be." The marquis spoke coldly but reasonably. The rich dark carriage rolled through the narrow, echoing streets of Brest.

"Are you certain . . . that I must go through with it?"

The marquis's eyes narrowed, and he nodded. "You've heard my final word, Alexandre."

Alexandre grimaced and shrugged.

"What can I do? I haven't any money."

The Beauharnais home on rue Thévenot was in a run-down and noisy neighborhood, and there were beggars in the street. Rose was glad to get inside and leave the outside behind. Now, on the second floor, she stared out of the fly-specked window at the tannery across the street. Columns of sickening yellow smoke curled over the broken slate roofs of the drab gray Paris street.

Alone with Mimi, Rose heaved a sigh. "Where am I?" she exclaimed. "This isn't at all what I saw in my dreams of Paris. I saw a magical city full of fountains and statues and parks and beautiful houses."

Mimi touched Rose's shoulder. "You have to make the best of this. Your mother and father are counting on you."

"Do I have to go through with it? This is a nightmare, Mimi. I thought Alexandre's family had money."

"Maybe they did, once upon a time."

Rose paused, then looked mischievously at Mimi. "Did you see the women's hair? Could you make mine look like that, Mimi?"

"The ladies here look like they have birdhouses on their heads. Sure, I can do that — but do you really want it?"

Rose threw up her hands. "I want to be like everyone

else — if I'm going to stay. The trouble is, I can't *speak* like them, *act* like them, or even *dress* like them."

Mimi turned away from the trunk she was unpacking. She joined Rose at the window. All about the room were piles of clothes that smelled so strongly of the sea, it felt as if they were still aboard ship.

"What's so bad out there?" Mimi asked as they looked at the long rows of identical houses. As far as the eye could see, the peaked roof buildings, jammed against one another, stretched all the way to the Seine in a haze of city smoke.

Rose wiped away a tear. "I don't think he likes me," she said.

"How could he not like you, Rose? He doesn't even know you." Mimi gave Rose a hug. "Don't fret, *ma jolie jeune fille*, that man will like you."

In bed that night, Rose listened to the strange creaking of the settling old house and the rumble of the late-night carts outside and the coarse voices of old men moving about their night soil and sewer work.

"He likes my money, Mimi," she said out of the blue.

Mimi giggled. "Your money? You mean a bunch of furniture and things back in Trois-Ilets? *Mon ange*, that's why you are marrying this man — so you and your family will *have* some money."

"They will say we're foreign and low mannered, these Parisians."

"Hold your head high. You'll be all right."

Rose sighed, "How can *this* be Paris?"

"Paris is in your heart —"

"*Mon coeur est en Martinique*," Rose whispered, and she imagined the sugar mill and the crickets and bats and moths, and the silky, warm way the air feels at night when you smell the burnt aroma of breadfruit cooking on an open fire, and the lowing of the cows in the guinea grass down by the meadow, and then she fell asleep dreaming of home.

In spite of herself, Rose could not help it — she was in love. It didn't matter that the man in question had no heart. He had *something*. She was taken in by that thing, whatever it was, swept away whenever she saw him, and miserable when he was gone.

When Alexandre came into the house in his white coat and leather boots, she shivered all over, praying he'd talk to her. But even she could see that he wasn't interested in her in the way she was interested in him.

Alexandre's wealthy friends thought the forthcoming marriage was ridiculous, or at best, amusing. They knew why he was doing it, however.

The duc de La Rochefoucauld asked him one day, "What does your dear little hummingbird *read?*"

Alexandre said, "I'm not aware that she reads anything. However, she likes being read to."

"How perfectly childlike," the duc remarked. "Does your Rose know the teachings of Monsieur Rousseau, whose *Social Contract* is on everyone's lips?"

Alexandre shrugged. "I haven't any idea about that — but I should think not. As I said, she doesn't read."

"Those charming Créoles," the duc said. "Island-born and -bred, like the sugar that precedes them, why, I am acquainted with these ladies of such exotic beauty." The duc poured himself some wine from a crystal decanter. "To tell the truth," he said, "the Créoles will one day take their place in the highest echelon of our society. But you must lead your little lady along, Alexandre. You must educate her. She's like a child who wants training."

Alexandre winced. "Do I look like a schoolmaster? And what is to be gained by putting a veneer on such rough wood?"

"Well," the duc replied, "perhaps your West Indian Rose has other, more appealing virtues."

Sad to say, Alexandre could think of none at that moment. He knew that she could read and write, and that she was an apt pupil. However, he said nothing of this to the duc.

F o u r

Paris, 1779

On a dark December day Rose and Alexandre signed the marriage contract that bound the betrothal. Rose was greatly relieved, as she had been afraid Alexandre would back out at the last minute.

Upon signing his name Alexandre sighed so loudly that the two lawyers who were present shifted in their seats and exchanged glances. However, no one in the family seemed to notice or care. Then it was Rose's turn to sign. Her hand shook and the goose quill seemed as heavy as lead. Her sigh, as it were, came from her hand's near refusal to write. Finally, though, it was done. The pen's reluctant point had stuck to every pulp in the paper, but Rose had completed her signature: *Marie-Josèphe Rose Tascher de La Pagerie.*

Afterward, Alexandre and Rose had a glass of punch. Yet after they touched glasses, his roving blue eyes rested everywhere but on her. Finally, to gain his attention for a moment she made a face.

"You don't like it?" he asked.

"It's sweet — and bitter. Is it worth the bother?"

Alexandre's right eyebrow raised. "The marriage or the drink?"

Rose wrinkled her nose. She wanted to say "both." For she knew the truth. Alexandre's signature was worth one hundred times the value of hers, but without hers it was worth nothing.

The best thing she had to offer was her aunt Edmée's gift of a house east of Paris in Noisy-le-Grand. The best thing he had to offer her was a glorious if slightly tarnished title. Soon she would be a vicomtesse. People would have to look up to her then.

Three days after the marriage contract was signed the wedding took place. Rose wore a satin dress trimmed with snowy lace. She had a towering headdress in front of which there was a misty veil. Lost under this equipage, Rose wore a corset that was too tight and a dress that was too heavy. She had a headache and was dizzy during the wedding.

Worst of all, her father, Joseph, was too sick to attend. He'd been sick ever since their arrival in France, and now he longed to go home but was too ill to do so.

Alexandre, dressed in a black silk coat, was at his stunning best, plus he was nice to her. Before the ceremony, he'd even said, "Here, Rose, I want you to have something to remember this day forever." He then gave her a pair of earrings that had little jewels in them, plus two bracelets and a diamond watch on a chain.

The presents thrilled Rose more than the wedding itself.

The ceremony, dizzy as it was for her, went by quickly, and was soon a memory neither joyous nor painful but something of each mixed together.

*　*　*

The season of winter parties came and went. Alexandre was always out. Rose was always in. "I see you're going out again," Rose remarked one evening. That day he'd promised to present her at Fanny de Beauharnais's popular salon. Fanny, Alexandre's novelist cousin, was dying to meet her. Naturally Rose was aching to meet Fanny, too, for to be seen at her salon was an immediate invitation to all the other fashionable events in Paris.

"Why shouldn't I go out alone if I want to?" Alexandre replied coldly.

"You should — but why don't you ever take me with you? Aren't we married? Isn't it good for us to be seen together?"

Alexandre gave her a condescending glance. "I am *seen* with the queen, Marie-Antoinette. Isn't that good for *us*?"

"For you, maybe."

"No, not for me. For my *career*."

Rose lowered her head. She fought back the tears. How well she knew what his career consisted of —

wasted nights among young officers of the regiment. Dancing and drinking until they fell off balconies.

She let him go, however. She always did. What else could she do?

It was a strange life she led as a vicomte's wife. Yes, as a vicomtesse, she was locked up in the Paris of her dreams — but all she could do was dream about it. She couldn't see it.

Her sad routine followed the same schedule day in and day out. Sleep until midday. Get up, sip coffee. For several hours, primp and powder and rouge her face into wakefulness while gossiping with Mimi. Then, after putting on a gown of gold with green stripes, she'd wrap herself in a fur robe, and go for a modest carriage ride with Aunt Edmée. She looked the part, but the role took her nowhere.

"You must go out more, *ma petite*," Edmée suggested as they toured the Champs-Élysées.

"With whom? You're the only one who takes me anywhere."

"Don't give up, *ma chérie*. You know men — or you should by now. Their needs are more selfish than ours — drinking, hunting, regimenting, and whatnot." Edmée gazed knowingly at Rose.

"I don't worry, Auntie, about Alexandre's regimenting or his drinking — it's his whatnot behavior, as you put it, that worries me."

"Oh, but you're sixteen — a girl still. Well, a girl-wife, to be exact. You've years ahead of you with Alexandre. You'll get to know his ways. . . ."

When Alexandre's six months of regimental duty were finished, he didn't bother to return home. His debts had mounted. So had his affairs. Now the seasons passed quietly for Rose. Alexandre came and went like the seasons themselves, bringing a brusque coldness or an unwelcome warmth into the house; and now Rose, six months pregnant, began to hate her home and her life. The stink of the tanneries, the sullen gentility of her in-laws, the woeful isolation, the continuing ill health of her father, all these made her feel she'd made a wrong turn by coming to France.

Only Mimi kept up Rose's spirits. Little else could.

One day Mimi told Rose, "A child will brighten your life and bring your husband back to your side. . . . As for the other things you mention, the things you don't like, do you think living at La Pagerie is better than what you have here? What hope would you ever have of becoming a vicomtesse on the little island of Martinique?"

To this, Rose said nothing. She knew Mimi was probably right. But that didn't not stop her from feeling used, downtrodden, and depressed. What earthly good was a title without a life to go with it?

Deep down she hated being a vicomtesse. She longed to swim in the river with the lilies that grew along the banks and the fish that nibbled at her toes.

When all else failed to amuse her, Mimi brought out her tarot deck. The fortune-telling cards that Rose was, day by day, becoming dependent upon always held her attention because they reminded her of the ancient fortune-teller Eliama and the prophecy she'd cast so long ago.

Why was it not working?

As Mimi shuffled images of the future and placed them on the low mahogany table, Rose forgot all about the mud-brown streets of sad, soulless Paris. The cards transported her to a fantastic place where time ceased to exist. The flutter of allegorical faces — King and Queen and even the ghastly grim Hanged Man, upside down and trying to smile, summoned moon-winged tropical moths into the room. The memory of hot, moist, mystic nights brought back the childhood smell of plantains frying and the Pagerie singing under the verandah.

Home again, amidst familiar sounds and fragrances, Rose was one with everything. And then even despair did not frighten her.

Sometimes, when drawing the Jester and seeing his belled hat and ear-to-ear grin, the two women laughed until tears coursed down their cheeks — tears of longing and lost sorrow, to which the only answer was laughter.

Alexandre was away when Rose's time came. The birth was not difficult, but her feeling of being alone made it seem harder than it was. When, at last, Alexandre showed up to see his son, he was pleased to name him Eugène-Rose. But that was the extent of his family sentiment. Directly he trotted off on a pleasure tour of Italy.

As the months of absence passed, Rose kept track of Alexandre's activities in her daily diary. She noted, for instance, that he'd been gone to Italy for eight months. Then, back briefly. Then gone again in September. No farewells, just disappearances in the dead of night. After a while, though, he wrote to her saying he was going to sail for America to fight the war against the British.

This news coincided with the fact that Rose was with child again.

In April when the poppies bloomed in Paris, Alexandre wrote again. The news was, as always, discouraging to her. He'd seen no active duty in America — for he hadn't even gone there! His far-reaching plan to visit the Americas had landed him in Martinique. From there he wrote Rose a long letter, which took her completely by surprise.

"He accuses me of being a loose woman, Mimi," she cried. "Me — a girl who was but sixteen! He says I was not a virgin when we met. Mimi, how could Alexandre say such things? He must be mad."

Mimi looked up from her sewing.

"What is not the truth cannot hurt, Rose. There's not a thread of truth in this blasphemy." Mimi held up her needle and the white thread that dangled from it. "His words are not even as thick as this," she vowed. "After all, I was there — and I should know!"

Rose had no idea what she could do against such willful slander. Immoral conduct, even falsely proven by a man, was a serious offense against a woman of good reputation. Worst of all, Alexandre drove home a dagger of despair: "Be out of there by the time I return," he wrote in a letter of such rancor that Rose gasped while reading it.

Under this dark cloud of apprehension, Rose's second child, a girl, was born. She named her Hortense.

There were but two courses of action for a wife thus scorned by a deceitful husband. If Alexandre had "proof," as he called it, she could contest the evidence. But he had bribed witnesses, people in Fort-Royal who had always been jealous of Rose's family.

She thought, *I know that he's bribed slaves to repudiate me. But there are few who would do me such unkindness. Nonetheless, their testimony may be believable. How can I present myself in my true and innocent light? Should I just be myself? Or will that go against me? Must I garner testimonies of my own?*

Once again, or perhaps as always, Rose was alone. She would have to make decisions about her future without the help of anyone but Edmée and Mimi. They stuck by her, of course. But what they could not tell her was how to fight a dragon. And that was indeed what her husband had turned into.

As for a place to live while she fought for her good

name, Rose was unsure about that, too. She could return to La Pagerie and live with her parents. Or she could go to Pentemont, a convent in Paris. Neither of these choices seemed right. But in the fall of that year Rose, for lack of a better idea, chose Pentemont.

Five

Paris, 1783

Rose gazed out of the second-story window of her new apartment in the old Paris abbey. Until a final settlement was made between Alexandre and herself, this was to be her home.

"How old are you?" asked the abbess of Pentemont.

"I'm twenty," Rose said, "but what does that matter?"

"You seem to have seen more than enough tribulation for one so young. Perhaps here at Pentemont, you can put your burdens behind you." The abbess gave her a kind smile.

"Is this so fine a place that it cures the heart as well as the head?" Rose asked. She looked around the small two-room apartment. The abbess did not answer her immediately, but she continued to smile sympathetically.

Rose took Eugene's hand and they studied the stone courtyard. The grounds were very beautiful. The autumn oaks were a deep brown, and the chestnut trees were laden with nuts. The gold dome of Les Invalides glittered over the tops of the trees.

The city seemed far away, but it was really quite near.

"Are there any tanneries nearby?" Rose asked uneasily.

The abbess shook her head, saying, "Heavens, no." Then she said, "The princesse de Condé was here today, and tonight you will dine with the duchesse de Monge and Madame de Creny. Do you know them?"

"I know *of* them."

The abbess went on in her soft, cheerful voice, "Our oysters are always fresh and so are the truffles. For those who like to linger by the fire after dinner, we have fine coffee and cognac. Do you think you will be able to make the requisite adjustment, Madame de Beauharnais?" The abbess smiled, and there was a gentle, mocking sparkle in her greenish-blue eyes.

"I believe so," Rose said, looking at Mimi, who sat in silence on Rose's trunk, the same one that had come from Martinique, and that had smelled of the sea when it had been opened four years earlier on their arrival in Paris. All of that seemed so long ago.

Eugène was crawling under the bed in the adjoining room. "I think I'll be all right at Pentemont," Rose told the abbess with that same wavering uncertainty in her voice. Then she added, "As content as women who haven't husbands are anywhere."

The abbess remarked, "Women without husbands seem to flourish at Pentemont. Anyway, we have many of them to keep you company."

After she'd taken leave of them, Mimi shook her head. "No husband is the least of your worries, Rose. No money, Hortense gone to a wet nurse, you, me, and Eugène gone to convent. Well, I suppose it could be worse."

"Yes," Rose put in, "I could be back in that paint-peeling, tannery-stinking house with beggars at the door and a husband who accuses me of infidelity. I say, be happy in the abbey, for it's liable to be as good as it gets in Paris."

"I'd rather eat oysters than lamb," Mimi added.

"But what I would give for a sweet mango," Rose said.

Eugène came out of the bedroom holding a big gold oak leaf between his thumb and his forefinger. He was twirling it around. "Look what just blew in the window," he said proudly.

Rose smiled at her son as she admired the leaf. "How I wish," she went on, "that little Hortense would blow in like this leaf. Don't you miss her, Eugène? Too bad about the convent's silly rules."

"I miss everyone," he answered. "Father, too."

"You can't miss what you don't have, my son."

Two years passed. Rose remained at Pentemont. As the abbess had predicted, she was content with the place. But her troubles were just mounting. Alexandre, who was constantly beset with debts, feuded with his father over his mother's estate. He fought with Rose as well, mostly over the terms of their separation. For Alexandre, his gambling debts were more important than his wife and children. Months went by with no word from him. When he sent Rose money, it was never enough.

One frosty February night, Alexandre came to Pentemont unexpectedly, and charmed his way through the front door. Rose stood holding a candle, wearing only a nightdress, while Alexandre begged a quick peek at his son's face before going back to the regiment. "You cannot know," he exclaimed, "how much I love that little boy. Can't I see him just for a moment?"

"Do you miss him as much as I miss Hortense?" Rose demanded.

"I'm sorry you don't get to see her as much as when we were together," he said softly. "But then I guess the convent has its rules."

"Alexandre, when were we *ever* together?"

At this he shrugged and walked into the dark toward Eugène's bed. A moment later, he returned with Eugène, sound asleep, bundled in a blanket in his arms.

"Where do you think you're going with my son?" Rose was nearly hysterical as she saw him move toward the door.

"My son!" Alexandre vowed, and he pushed Rose out of his way, then charged long-legged down the stairs.

Rose and Mimi ran after him. But to no avail. His coach was waiting for him outside, and they watched as he thundered off in a cloud of new-fallen snow.

There was nothing for Rose to do but break down. Her precious boy was gone. She had nothing left to live for. She was broke, her children were gone, and her husband hated her. Collapsing into Mimi's arms, Rose released the pent-up pain of months of mute suffering. She cried herself into a senseless rage. Nor was there an end to it. After that cold kidnapping night, Rose didn't hear from Alexandre again.

The only thing that relieved the suffering she felt

was the daily progress she made in her suit for a legal separation from the man who had so terribly wronged her.

Fortunately, Rose now had a much stronger basis for a suit. Kidnapping was a serious charge. And despite Alexandre's status and charm, his irrational actions weren't going to be overlooked by a magistrate. He'd been caught in his own web. Thus Rose built her case with an advocate and bided her time until Alexandre should be served his summons. The certainty that she'd been wronged and that he would eventually have to pay kept Rose from losing her mind for the next few weeks.

Fontainebleau, France,
1785

After the separation was settled, Eugène was returned by court order to the convent. Rose forgot to be angry at Alexandre, even though he once again neglected his required five-thousand-*livre*-per-year payments. Everyone else in the family was furious with him, but she and her children were not. The only thing she dreaded was the day when Alexandre was legally permitted to take Eugène away to be educated. This was to happen on Eugène's fifth birthday.

Rose's nature was very forgiving. Even while she endured personal poverty, there was a place in her heart for this luckless nobleman who'd once stepped royally out of a coach in Brest to meet an impressionable young

Créole girl. In some strange and inexplicable way, Rose was joined to Alexandre by a myth of false but lasting beauty. This romantic notion stuck with her regardless of the consequences.

But when, after two years' time, Alexandre showed up to take Eugène, Rose was beside herself.

"I did not expect this visit to come so soon," Rose said.

"You mean, you didn't expect me? But our written agreement spells out the exact date when I would come and get Eugène. His education awaits him. Why waste more words over this? This time it's perfectly legal and binding."

Rose's voice faltered. "But . . . Alexandre . . . he's only five! I thought you would take him . . . later on."

Clinging to his pet cat, Eugène came timidly into the drawing room of the apartment. For a moment, he studied the man in white, the tight leggings, the knee-high boots, the dove-gray coat. Eugène's face showed more surprise than fear. He hadn't seen his father in a long while.

Alexandre came forward, his sword scabbard ringing against his thigh. "Come along, Eugène." Alexandre took the boy's small hand in his own. A moment later, the soldier, the little boy, and the cat were gone.

The door closed behind them.

Then it opened.

Alexandre tossed the cat inside, and closed the door again.

Now he was gone for the last time.

Seven

Toulon, 1788~1790

The next two years passed eventfully for Rose. With Mimi and Hortense she returned to Martinique. There she saw her mother and father and sister for what was likely to be the last time. Things were not the same on the little island of her birth, for, as in France, the Revolution was already under way. The slaves were attempting to overthrow the rich planters, and a war had broken out between them.

Fearing for their lives, Rose, Hortense, and Mimi fled the island only to hear onboard the ship the dreaded rumors of the Revolution in France. When they arrived in Toulon, the first thing Rose noticed was that there were no more flags with the Bourbon fleur-de-lys. Gone was any flapping remembrance of the falling monarchy.

Only the revolutionary colors — red, white, and blue — could be found in the bustling, bannered streets. On the sides of coaches and from every window in every building, even from the raised hands of running children, there were the blazing colors of the mad onrushing Revolution.

Wearing the same tatty, flea-ridden clothes they'd worn for seven weeks of sea voyage, the woebegone threesome came to dry land, thankful to be alive.

After refreshing themselves at an inn by eating a steaming mussel stew, Rose counted out the last *sous* she had. There wasn't quite enough to get back to Paris.

Rose lifted her wineglass, smiled, and said to Mimi, "I'm still a vicomtesse — am I not?"

Mimi gave her a vacant stare. "Who knows what you are anymore," she said.

The meal of mussels, pork loin cooked with apples, and hard bread returned them to a greater sense of well-being than they had known in months. Even though the unknown lay hard upon her, Rose was glad to be back in

France. She wanted to see Eugène. How he must have grown in the last two years. Thinking of the longed-for reunion with her son, Rose pushed away the thought that she hadn't sufficient carriage fare to return.

"Look, Maman," Hortense cried when they finally got passage on a mail coach that would take them part-way to Paris. Hortense's freshly washed blond hair was braided and ribboned. She looked no worse for the long trip at sea. Her small face was brown from the sun, and her blue eyes were as bright as berries.

Rose glanced out the window.

Hortense pressed against her. "Maman, the mountains are burning."

"There, there, *ma petite*." The carriage rocked on and Rose said, "You're going to see your brother soon — won't he be big?"

Hortense rubbed her eyes. "How big?"

Rose spread her arms far apart. "He'll be as broad as an ox."

Hortense started to giggle.

On a great hill above the road was a castle. Columns of smoke leaked out of every cornice and crevice.

There was another passenger traveling with them, a bootier by trade. "You will see soon enough, *citoyenne*, that things are different in France." The man spoke and had a world-weary smile that never left his face.

Rose felt the coach lurch. There followed a hard and sudden bump. The bootier groaned. "These roads have been torn up by the troops," he said, grimacing. He adjusted his striped linen tunic. "Why should I complain?" He fanned himself vigorously with his cap, and went on, "How can I? The soldiers' boots are made by me." He chuckled noisily.

Rose noticed that the bootier's tunic looked like the red, white, and blue flags she'd seen in Toulon, only this one was cut into a buttonless shirt. "If I may be so bold, who *are* you, sir?" Rose asked. The coach wheel struck a stone and sent it ricocheting into the night. Hortense, now sleeping on Rose's lap, reached out with her hands in the dark. "Go back to sleep, *mon enfant*," Rose whispered, stroking Hortense's forehead.

The bootier replied to Rose's question. "My tannery is near Coeur-de-Miracle. My bootery is at the front of the same building."

"I know exactly where that is, *and* what it smells like."

"By the way, you mustn't *sir* me anymore."

"No?"

"*Certainement pas*. We no longer call ourselves by titles — just *citoyen et citoyenne*, citizen and citizeness."

Darkness streamed by the windows of the coach. The burning castle was gone. The cold fragrance of pine came in the open windows. Rose sighed and stretched her legs. The coach went rumbling past small farms with comforting barnyard smells.

The bootier continued his harangue.

"The fight for liberty is *not* what is so irksome, *citoyenne*. But rather, the lack of humility. The street rabble who've taken over — they're . . ." He paused to choose the right words.

"Please continue, sir, I mean, *citoyen*." The word seemed so odd and unworthy to Rose. *I wonder if I will ever get used to it. It sounds like I am acting in a play.*

The bootier leaned forward. His breath stank of stale wine.

Rose melted back into the leather seat to get away from him.

"Don't be afraid, *citoyenne*. I want to reveal some-thing — something of a private nature."

"Say it outright," Rose told him. "You've nothing to hide from me or Mimi."

The bootier flinched. "You've been away, I see."

"Yes, that is true."

Suddenly, the little pinched-faced man put his face in his hands, and his shoulders began to shake.

Hortense sat up and said, "What's wrong? Is some-thing the matter?"

"Lie down, *ma chérie*. Nothing's wrong."

The bootier wiped his eyes on his sleeve. "Forgive me," he said. Rose could barely make him out. It was dark now and Rose saw his face only in shadow.

"Forgive me, *citoyenne*," he begged. "I know who you are. Some time ago, I would pass you on the street and doff my buckled hat. Do you remember? No, I see you do not. Well, that is as it is — or rather was." His voice became faint. "You being a vicomtesse, and myself a mere bootier. But now, such words are gone, swept away as by a terrible storm. We're equals now. Sad to say." He swallowed and sighed.

Rose was surprised. "But how do you know who I am?"

The bootier became animated again. The hollows of his face were suddenly illumined by the torches of some men fishing off a bridge.

"Citoyenne de Beauharnais, your husband is the new president of the National Assembly. I used to make his boots for him — now I repair them." He gave a short, ironic laugh, ending in a cough. "We repair *everything* now," he went on. "That is all we do anymore, repair what has been ruined."

"Is it really so bad?" Rose asked.

The bootier coughed. "Who knows?" he said with a little shrug. "We're too much in it to really see it for what it is. The intent isn't bad — to democratize our world. It's the way we go about it that's awful."

Rose looked puzzled. "How so?"

The bootier said, "We go about it with a sharp knife. Whoever disagrees dies. I myself did not hate royalty all that much."

Rose tried to imagine Alexandre as president. Inwardly, she smiled. He was born to importance, Alexandre was. Fashioned for it. *And so,* she thought, *the Revolution has been kind to my former husband. I wonder, will it be kind to me?*

Eight

Paris, 1791

They had found a barge that brought them right up the Seine. A few sunny days on the river had done them no harm, and probably a lot of good. But the first thing Rose noticed on her return to Paris was that there were no more beautiful clothes. Instead the people wore tricolor tunics, as she'd seen in Toulon. These ragged outfits looked like leftover costumes from a comic opera. Wigs and ruffled lace were no more. Perfumes, powders, and pomades were also gone, which meant the people smelled of worry and sweat now, and the city itself was coated in smoky grime from the fires that had been lighted in the streets.

It was a very discouraging sight — Paris, down-at-the-heels, begging for bread. However, Rose was not without hope — or contacts. Her estranged husband was now a prestigious figure, a golden boy, one of the "fabulous forty-seven." This was a group of liberal nobles who were essentially running the whole country. Fanny de Beauharnais, who had grown to be Rose's close friend before she'd left for Martinique, was one of the most popular novelists in Paris.

So, when Rose got back into town with Hortense and Mimi, and they'd nowhere to go, she turned to Fanny, whose home on rue de Tournon was not far from the river. Outside, rats roamed the streets by the thousands. They were followed by half-starved cats, which, in turn, were stalked by feral dogs. Yet the predators were out-numbered by the vermin, which filled attics and cellars with their migrant squeaking. No place was safe from them; the rats ruled.

And mud reigned supreme. The rains had been heavy, and the streets were clogged with sewage and puddles that were as deep as lakes. Yet these were now patrolled by enterprising men called gutterleapers. For a fee they carried passersby piggyback from one side of the street to the other. Rose had no money, of course, and the gutterleapers didn't accept credit on anyone's name. So Rose and Mimi took turns carrying Hortense. Slowly they sloshed their way to Fanny's door.

Fanny threw open the door when Rose dropped the brass knocker.

"No beggars. We've nothing for you!" Fanny shouted.

"Fanny — it is me, Rose. We're just back from Martinique."

Fanny's mouth dropped open. The truth was, she didn't recognize any of these mud-drenched, sewage-smelling people. Nor did they recognize Fanny, whose hair had gone snowy white and was quite uncombed. Rouge reddened her cheeks to the brightness of a ripe red apple. She looked like an actress gone to seed and out of work.

Rose looked like a gutterleaper, as did Mimi and Hortense. But after a moment or two of convincing talk, they were let in.

"Oh, *mon dieu*, Rose, you've missed absolutely *everything*! We've gone from diamonds to dirt. We're as poor as can be. Living off my royalties. Still, we keep up appearances as best as we can."

They didn't embrace — for obvious reasons — and Rose and company were hastened to the rear of the house, where a cauldron of water was heated for their baths.

Later, scrubbed almost to the bone, they emerged in clothes Fanny had provided for them.

"We're still half starved," Rose admitted, "but at least we're clean now."

"Don't ever say 'hungry' *in this house*!" Fanny cried. "We'll feed you right now."

She had a poor prince and his wife — Fanny called them Prince and Princesse, as if they had no other names — working for her. That was her entire staff.

They went to the kitchen to prepare a board and returned with a loaf of long, hard, crusty bread, some good, salty cheese, and a tureen of potato soup. Rose, Mimi, and Hortense wasted no time falling upon this meal, which was placed upon a broad tabletop with a well-worn and stained tablecloth.

"You eat like wolves," Fanny remarked. Then she sighed and said, "We still have our crystal, and our wine cellar is as well stocked as ever." So saying she poured out four glasses of red table wine. "Now that you're back," Fanny asked, "what do you most want to do?"

"I can't wait to see Eugène," Rose said. "Even if it's just for a short time."

"We'll pick him up from military school tomorrow," Fanny promised. "You won't believe how big he's gotten and how well he's done. He's a regular military man now."

Although the Revolution was in full swing, it didn't stop Fanny from writing a new novel. "My novels sell less well than the daily broadsheets," she confessed to Rose, "but they do support us."

Broadsheet newspapers were all the rage. Everyone wanted to know the latest news. One day the king and the queen were hauled out of town in disgrace, and the papers were full of it. People sat in the cafés all day, reading and discussing the latest political vagary.

Up and down it went, and no one knew which end was up. All at once, as fast as Marie-Antoinette and her husband, Louis the fourteenth, were whisked out of town, suddenly, and with no apologies, they were brought back and put in place at Tuileries, and all the papers were telling how they toasted the republican order and the great new reformer Maximilien Robespierre. Known all over Paris as "The Incorruptible," he alone seemed to be the force of the future, the leading man of France. And even the king and queen acknowledged it.

The following summer the air was very hot and the Seine was perfectly still. Rose, tired of the city, took Mimi, Hortense, and Eugène to a country cottage in

Croissy that was owned by a friend of her father's, Désirée Hosten.

In Paris, now, the Law of Suspects was posted on every public building. This dreaded law stated, "*Anyone is suspect who, by their conduct, their connections, their remarks, or their writings, show themselves the partisans of tyranny.*"

"Outrageous," Désirée exclaimed. "All of us are being watched. You must have a certificate to show your republican standing — or else."

"Or else what?" Rose queried.

"To prison — or worse."

"In Croissy, I have only to ask my friend Henri, a national agent who is an informer for the Committee of General Security." Désirée sighed. "Oh, the futility of it all — committees and securities and who knows what!" She sucked her teeth. "What a disgrace!"

"But can this fellow you mention get our papers in order?"

"He can, and he will."

Thus the documents were procured and properly stamped, and for the moment, Rose felt somewhat secure. Then came the order from the National Assembly: "All children must, to keep their status as good citizens, be trained as tradesmen."

So Eugène, at eleven years of age, was quickly apprenticed to a cabinetmaker and nine-year-old Hortense was apprenticed as a seamstress. There was a little money coming in from Alexandre, but just enough for a kitchen maid named Agatha and the bread and wine that kept the little family alive. All together there were six people, plus Désirée and her daughter, under one roof. Madame Lannoy was brought in to teach Hortense the art of sewing, and she seconded as a governess. Life seemed to be a little better in Croissy than it had been in Paris.

"I have good news — but maybe not for *you*," Agatha said one morning to Rose.

Rose often heard such statements from Agatha, but she was not used to it. "We're a republican family, Agatha. No different from anyone else."

Agatha replied, "Well, what I want to say is, the king's time on earth is almost done."

"What are you talking about?"

"They've got him in prison," Agatha said with a smile that betrayed her bad teeth. "Him and his wife. They're in the Tower. Even the children, and whenever they let the bunch of them go out for a walk in the courtyard, people throw stones at them. The guillotine's next — everyone says so."

Rose questioned, "Why are you so cheerful about it, Agatha? The poor people. The poor children. There's no end of sorrow I feel for them."

Agatha chirped, "Don't say those things on the street, *citoyenne*, or you'll be in the Carmelite prison yourself."

Rose looked at the slow-moving Seine beyond the open window of the house. "If that is where we are destined to go, then there's little I can do about it, is there?"

The quiet months in Croissy lingered on, however.

Summer turned to fall. The chestnuts dropped from the trees and were roasted. The people hunted morels in the parks. Then, suddenly, the false summer was over. It was winter. And the cold was so harsh, the sparrows fell dead from the iced branches of trees, and wolves crept into the Tuileries, the palace garden, and howled mournfully at night.

The letters from Martinique took longer than ever to reach Paris. There was now an English blockade and the British were at war with France. Finally a letter came from Claire de Tascher. Her news was devastating. Rose learned that her father had died one month after she'd left Martinique. Her sister Manette had passed on twelve months later. The sugar mill had been spared, and Claire was there with the few slaves who'd stayed on.

With tears running down her face, Rose composed a letter to her mother. Paris news was no better except that no immediate family had perished. The king and queen were guillotined, their headless bodies ridiculed in the streets. The dauphin, the king's heir to the throne, was in prison. It was rumored that his sister had left the country. All the monarchists were arrested, executed, or had run off to England, Italy, and Germany. Edmée and the marquis had somehow managed to stay out of sight, and therefore hadn't been jailed yet; neither had Fanny, though Rose wasn't sure where any of them were hiding.

There were regular night searches, and the houses were turned upside down as governmental agents sought any evidence that would lead to an arrest. Anything could be used against someone with a title. The tribunal court of death was processing people by the hundreds. Rose didn't say in her letter to Claire that she awaited the knock on her own door — that she felt it coming. She didn't say that she woke up in the nights hearing a pounding on her door. She didn't say she almost longed for it so that the waiting would be over.

Paris, 1794

According to Maximilien Robespierre, the republic needed only one thing to perfect it: a good, honest "bleeding." The nation, he said, needed to be cleansed like a sick person who was mercifully bled by a physician.

In the next six months eight thousand human heads would fall; each day the count climbed higher. Yet no one would deny the republic was not the better for the bleeding. The murdering in the middle of the night went on. The gutters sang with blood as red as wine.

During the month of April, anyone related to a noble became an immediate enemy of the people. Thus Alexandre was captured and sent to the Carmelite prison to await his sentence.

Rose was in the greatest of danger.

Late one night the deputies for the Committee for Public Safety came to the little house in Croissy. In no time they found a letter from Alexandre, the acknowledged traitor. By association, Rose was guilty of treason. No use protesting that only a few weeks earlier Alexandre had been a national hero fighting for the glory of France. His prominence as well as his eminence in the registry bloodlines marked him for death.

So Rose and Désirée Hosten, her hostess, were taken to the convent of the Carmelites known as Les Carmes. Eugène and Hortense were left — for the moment — with Mimi, who knew better than anyone how to hide. That was Rose's only consolation — her children being left in the care of Mimi, whose African ancestry made her safer than the average Frenchman.

The torchlighted tunnels of Les Carmes did a macabre dance as the two women entered the prison. Graffiti written in blood covered the walls that briefly flared before them as they walked, cowed and scared, to their cell.

The smell of death and decay. Gaunt women with shorn heads, women who were ageless because of their grief. The young were ancient and the ancient were young, or so it seemed to Rose. Men with whittled or missing ears kept popping up, grinning like jesters. These things filled Rose's eyes with horror as she walked along, her mouth clamped shut against the rotten air. Unwashed bodies soaked in desperate sweat.

Frightened, Rose and Désirée moved behind their jostling, humming jailer. And thus they passed through the cavern of the September Massacres. Here, six months earlier, judges in butcher's aprons, arms tattooed with tradesmen's logos, condemned seven thousand human beings to the guillotine, that terrible instrument of the republic.

The smell of it, the feel of it — the presence of death's tarot — bloomed before Rose's eyes as she proceeded down the shadow-splashed, blood-bathed halls where her footfalls and Désirée's echoed through that endless passage. At last their cell presented itself. Alexandre, pale and courteous, was there to greet them.

For Rose there was no more waiting for that frightful midnight knock on the door. For her and the others, the only knock left was the guillotine.

In a tiny, straw-strewn, urine-soaked cell, Rose resigned herself to a fate she'd only recently foreseen.

And then, as the days dragged gruesomely by, her faith in Mimi was rewarded. Eugène and Hortense proved they were alive and very close by. Moreover, with Mimi's help they found a secret way to get messages to Rose. This was accomplished by none other than Fortuné, the little pug that Alexandre had once given to Rose and the children. Now Fortuné became a canine messenger. Rose's heart leaped whenever she saw Fortuné's flat dark face and corkscrew tail show up in her cell.

As fate would have it, the surly turnkey who kept watch over the women had a soft spot for dogs — particularly pugs. Rose thought it was because he looked like one himself. But in any case, he let Fortuné come and go as if he lived there.

Hidden under Fortuné's collar were letters from Eugène telling Rose what was going on outside the walls of Les Carmes.

Rose learned through these letters that Eugene was a worthy apprentice who would one day be a "useful citizen of the republic." Hortense was a proper seamstress, he wrote. Madame Lannoy and Mimi were taking care of the children and she had managed to find Fanny. Agatha — no one knew where she was. He described how Fanny's servant, the prince, slipped out at night and caught cats, who sometimes had rats in their mouths —"and Maman, both the cats and the rats go into the family stew pot!"

Eugène wrote about the best as if it were the worst and the worst as if it were the best, which was exactly how Rose felt, too. There was no other way to live and breathe in such topsy-turvy conditions.

Anything could happen — and did.

However, the slightest mention of food — even the

flesh of felines — made Rose's mouth water. In the weeks, and then months, that passed, she grew light-boned and skeletal. One day Mimi got the princess to bake a bread braid, which looked so much like a collar that she and Fanny wrapped it around Fortuné's neck.

And the clever little dog ran to the prison without eating it!

That day Rose received Fortuné with tears in her eyes. She shared her cell with Désirée, the duchesse d'Aguillon, and Thérèse de Fontenay. All were starved. Rose refused to eat the braid of bread alone. So, small though it was, she divided it equally among the four of them.

"Have faith in me," Thérèse de Fontenay said after they'd eaten the last crumb of bread. Then she drew a crumpled paper from her bosom and handed it to Rose. "This piece of paper will condemn Robespierre," Thérèse explained in anger. Inscribed in Thérèse's own blood, the letter was addressed to her lover, Tallien.

Rose read aloud, "In eight days I will be a free

woman and the wife of Tallien, who will have freed the world of the murderer Robespierre. Or else I shall mount the scaffold with a curse for the cowardly."

Rose read the letter over and over. When she handed it back to her fellow prisoner, she remarked, "What if, through some mishap, Robespierre should get the letter?"

Thérèse shook her head. Harshly, she said, "Tallien, not Robespierre, shall receive it!"

"How can you be sure?"

"You have a dog who delivers letters and bread, and you can ask such a question? Isn't there some hope in your heart, Rose?"

Rose sank onto her cot. "This morning I saw the posting of names," she told her friends. "Alexandre's name was on that death warrant."

"Ah," said Thérèse, "so that's it." Her huge dark eyes were filled with sadness.

Rose gazed at her friend, the prettiest of all Parisian women. Robespierre, who hated physical beauty, had locked up Thérèse simply for looking lovely. Good looks, he thought, were the mark of the aristocracy. Down with them and all the corrupt things they stood for.

"Have faith," Thérèse whispered. Then she and Rose clung to one another in a strong embrace. "Have faith," Thérèse repeated. "I am sending my message today by a secret courier. Trust me, Tallien knows that Robespierre is plotting to kill him. When he sees my blood letter, Tallien will act at once. I promise you that, *ma chère* Rose."

Two days later Alexandre de Beauharnais was led to the scaffold. His fair head was put on the block, his curls were tied back, and then the blade was dropped. His headless body was tossed into a cart, the head rolling into the street where a child picked it up and pitched it in with the pile of bodies. While the cart creaked through the streets, the sewers piped tunefully with the blood of nobility and commoner alike.

The day Alexandre died, Rose fell ill and drifted in and out of a coma. On the ninth day she awoke just as the turnkey entered her cell. Roughly, he rolled her off her cot. She fell onto the hard stone floor that was strewn with rotten straw.

Thérèse helped Rose to her feet. "Are you giving this bed to another prisoner?" she asked the turnkey.

The coarse-faced, heavyset man nodded. "Citoyenne Beauharnais won't need a bed much longer."

Duchesse d'Aguillon protested, "She's nearly recovered — don't you see?"

"Recovered, eh?" The jailer snorted his disgust. "Well, let's hope she recovers in time to mount the scaffold." He spat on the moldy straw and wiped his stubbly chin.

"Be calm, my friends," Rose said. Her eyes gleamed with a strange, inner light.

The turnkey chuckled. "You'll be dead soon enough, *citoyenne*. Why don't you hurry up so you can join your fancy husband?"

"I'm not going to die," Rose said.

In her mind, buzzing like a hummingbird through the

gloomy twilit trees of Martinique, she saw below her an old woman sitting on the goose-pecked grass in the evening shadows. The old woman looked up into the air and smiled at the hummingbird as it soared past her head.

Rose moved her lips slowly. "I am going to live. Not only live," she said radiantly, "but one day *rule*."

"What's that?" Thérèse asked. She wiped the cold sweat off Rose's face with her dress.

"I shall be . . . *more* than a queen," Rose said clearly, her eyelids shut.

The turnkey left.

Rose opened her eyes. "I swear it shall be so," she said.

"I swear you'll be without a head soon," the turnkey shouted from behind the barred door.

Rose sat up and lifted her legs over the cot and onto the floor. Unsteadily, she stood up. Then she slowly made her way to the single window of the stone cell.

In the courtyard below was a woman in a dark red robe. She was gesturing with her hands. Clutching the crimson robe, she let it fall. She did this over and over while staring hopefully up at the window. The pantomime was repeated several times. At last, the woman completed it by swiping two fingers across her throat.

Rose turned to face her friends, who stood next to her. "Did you see that?"

They nodded in silence.

"But what does it mean?" Thérèse asked.

"It means," Rose explained, "that Robespierre is dead. Don't you see? The woman raised her robe, and then let it fall. She was trying to say, 'The Robe has fallen.' Don't you see, the bloody *Robe* has fallen," Rose said, her eyes shining. "Robespierre is *dead*," she cried when still no one seemed to understand — or to believe.

All at once, Thérèse became ecstatic. "It's come to pass," she cried. "Tallien, my wonderful, brave Tallien, has done the deed!"

The turnkey looked into the cell with a glum, disgruntled face. "Are you the new queen of France?" he said mockingly. "Or is that office filled by your friend who isn't going to die?"

Ten

Paris, 1794~1795

Thérèse was the first to go free. One day after the death of Robespierre, the news was all over Paris, and Thérèse was escorted out of Les Carmes by the order of Jean Tallien. He was now the people's hero, the new Incorruptible. "Don't worry," Thérèse told Rose and the duchesse. "I'll be back for both of you."

Rose couldn't help shedding tears, however, when she saw her dear friend depart. She and the duchesse had their faces pressed to the bars of the window as Therèse walked out into the sunlight, a free woman. But before disappearing around the corner, she turned and waved one last time to her friends.

Thérèse de Fontenay, who was soon to be Citoyenne Tallien, kept her word. Three days after she'd gone free, she returned with an order from Tallien, president of the Committee for Public Safety. His signature demanded the immediate release of Rose and the duchesse. Three thousand prisoners still remained, among them Désirée Hosten and so many others that Rose knew personally.

It was August. The summer sun was so bright, Rose could hardly see the three haunted figures standing before the prison gate. They shimmered in the sun's glare, the three fusing into one.

Then they became separate again.

Squinting, she could see who they were. Mimi, Eugène, and Hortense. Waiting for her on the corner.

Rose met them like a shadow, a quivering shade from Les Carmes suddenly brought out into the bright light of day.

Was this what it felt like to be free?

"Maman! Maman!" Hortense cried out.

"My poor Rose!" Mimi uttered with a sigh.

Eugène, speechless and shy, was trembling as much

as his mother, but he held himself as erect as his father would have, and at last, he threw his arms around her, feeling the thinness of her bones, the smallness of her frail frame.

Then they walked down the rue de Belle Chasse, and soon the ghastly prison named Les Carmes was no more.

In the months that followed, thousands of prisoners were sprung from their cells, and the death warrants of Robespierre were burned and the prison doors flung open. Only the guillotine remained, along with the ghosts who hovered over it and thickened the air, people said, all around it. The big blade stayed, rusting in the summer rain.

Once again, Rose made herself at home at Fanny's on rue de Tournon. There, in spite of all the adversity, Fanny had created a unique salon that was very popular. Officers, members of the Committee for Public

Safety, and emigrées who'd escaped the guillotine and returned to France gathered to toast the sublime Convention, the reorganized new government of France.

Paris was wearing fresh clothes once again. The streets were full of crazy entertainment. There were all kinds of theaters, cafés, and dance halls. The spirit of Paris was once again free and loose. Its circuslike streets ran with all types of people, trading and selling, hustling and bustling. Its air was full of the smell of lye from the tanneries mixed with the exotic new perfumeries and the mingled odors of mulch and mildew, rotten fish, and sewer water. Kitchens baking cheap bread layered the air with a rotten potato smell. A million breeds of unknown and newly minted mold came from freshly dug graves, festering sores, and the walking dead who had no idea they were dying.

Parisian women now had a fondness for the Ro-manesque — gowns that were open in front, sandals that laced to the knee, hair all garlanded and ivied and given the wife-of-Caesar look. Garden parties took place on flower-filled rafts, but there were also graveyard parties where the white-faced living communed with the blue-faced dead. People pretended to be dead and alive at the same time.

Altogether, Paris was a joyously insane city celebrating life, liberty, and the pursuit of parties.

Rose told Mimi that anything was better than *citoyen* and *citoyenne*. "Long live *monsieur et madame!*" she added.

"And powdered wigs!" Mimi said, laughing.

"And silk stockings!"

"And tangerine hair!"

"But what are we to make of it?" Rose wondered aloud. "The ground's still wet with the blood of Marie and Louis, and crazy people are dancing in the clothes those poor royals discarded."

"The dancing dead," Mimi remarked.

"So true," Rose agreed. "We all think we're half alive or half dead. Either way, I won't wash away my grief with wine or powder my face into forgetfulness or wear wigs that hide my gray hairs."

At a salon gathering that same night, Thérèse asked Rose, "Why do you think I'm wearing a wig the color of a boiled crayfish?" She arched her eyebrows and her pretty dark-brown eyes gleamed.

Politely, Rose gave a little shrug.

"I have at least one gray hair for every day I spent at Les Carmes," she lamented.

"Well, I never went there," Fanny said, "but I went white just the same." Her own head was covered in a wig the color of indigo.

Rose told the two of them, "You can't hide years, *mes amies*. You can only put your best foot forward — that is, if you still have a shoe to hang on it." Fanny extended an elegant foot encased with a gold-stitched calfskin slipper that winked in the candlelight. The three women laughed and their heads touched affectionately.

"I suppose being well shod is the best revenge for all those months in prison," Rose said with a brave smile. Then she asked, "Who is that funny little man over there?" The three women followed Rose's gaze across the crowded salon. "The one standing by Fortunée Hamelin."

Fanny said, "He is a general but he cuts a pretty poor figure, doesn't he? I've stood next to him when his hair was quite unwashed and he stank of gunpowder, body odor, and who knows what else. His haggard, gloomy looks make you think of a man you'd not want to meet in the dark. Or is that just me?"

"I just want to know his name," Rose said.

"This week he calls himself B-o-n-a-p-a-r-t-e." Thérèse spelled out the man's name.

"Last week," said Fanny, "he spelled it B-u-o-n-o-p-a-r-t-e."

Rose, still intrigued by the little general, asked, "Does he change his spelling to suit his mood?"

"Well," chuckled Thérèse, "the first spelling is, of

course, Italian, and as your little general hails from Corsica, I suppose he's more Italian than anything else."

"He's not *my* little general," Rose objected with a laugh.

"He could be — if you wanted him," Fanny put in.

The three women smiled.

That night, Rose lay awake with her head on a silk pillowcase. The hum of the evening's activities was still buzzing in her head. Once again, she imagined the curious man who'd so strangely caught her attention. He hadn't moved, yet everyone in the salon had moved around him. Part of the time, he read palms — to anyone who offered one for his inspection, and to quite a few who didn't.

When the general had looked into Rose's palm, he'd drawn a sudden breath. Momentarily, his eyes had met hers, and she'd felt her heart jump. His penetrating gray eyes were large — and deep. Like grayish-blue stones at the bottom of a fast-moving stream.

The general's gaze held her fast. She couldn't move. She couldn't think. He had her hooked.

Now those same hypnotic eyes were following her to sleep.

How strange, she thought before drifting off. *He never said a word about my future. What did he see in my palm? Something? Nothing? Everything?*

The Sword

Eleven

Paris, 1795

Rose's new home at 6 rue de Chantereine was a mansion in miniature. A long drive fronted it, and a carriage house, with stable and garden, completed it. The house was set back from the tawdry road and run-down neighborhood by an encircling hedge, which gave the place an aura of mystery.

She now had a cook, a gatekeeper, a groom, and four household helpers, including Madame Lannoy and Mimi. She owned a coach with two fine black Hungarian horses.

For once, Rose was set for life — or so it seemed.

However, no one knew how she'd achieved this rise in status in so short a time. Even Rose wondered how she'd done it.

"I still don't understand," Fanny said, turning in an awestruck semicircle as she regarded Rose's salon for the first time.

"So," Rose explained, "I need but two things: a gardener and a coachman. Then I'll have everything."

"But how in the world did you pay for all this?" Fanny asked her, still looking with admiration, and perhaps a little envy, at the blue and silver room, which glittered with plushly appointed furniture, potted palms, tapestries, and deeply folded velvet drapes. The wallpaper had country scenes of hunts and huntsmen, and the floors were of burnished wood shined to a golden hue. The whole place glowed with a richness that Fanny savored from every angle . . . and still her wonderment gave her no rest. How did a poverty-stricken widow with two children and no money manage to pull this off?

"You know as well as I do where the money comes from. Paul Barras pays for everything. I have nothing, really, except what he gives me. But that's more than enough."

"Is Paul *that* rich?"

"He's got ways and means," Rose answered evasively.

Fanny shook her head and smiled. "He must have received an inheritance then. The Paul I used to know wasn't that well off."

"Can you keep a secret?"

"You know I can't."

The two women burst out laughing.

Then after a pause, Rose said, "Paul's the most powerful man in France. That's all anyone needs to know."

Fanny nodded, frowned, and shook her head again. "That doesn't make him the *richest* one, though, does it?"

"All right, the truth . . ."

"Do tell." Fanny's eyes narrowed.

Rose confessed openly, "Paul buys and sells military goods: boots, food, arms, and almost anything that an army needs when it's on the move. He's a middleman, buying cheaply and selling high, and making fabulous profits."

Fanny sighed and said, "Oh, no. So, what *duties* does M. Barras require of you?" she winked impishly.

"Well, Paul likes his parties — so do I. Simple as that."

Rose saw that she wasn't going to shake off Fanny so easily. No one ever did. "Paul says I'm his *official* hostess."

"A title *and* a salary, you can't ask any more than that."

Still, Rose knew there was more to the tale than party management. She and Barras had become quite good friends. Tall and dark, Paul Barras was neither handsome nor magnetic, but something of the two emerged in the unholy orbit of his Parisian indulgences. All he did was business, and yet he was no businessman. He had money, but no one knew where it came from. He was mysterious. And his parties that began at dusk and ended at sunrise did little to make him less so.

Barras, Barras. Everybody spoke of him. But no one knew him. Except the little Corsican general who was often seen in his presence. Together they were an odd pair — the tallness and the shortness of them — laughable. Barras, impeccable in his dress. Bonaparte, threadbare and sloppy. And yet people said they were up to something, those two — like the Aesop fable of the fox and the cat, they had schemes and dreams, not one of which was known to anyone. Were their plans sinister?

Onto this carousel of questionable morality, Rose had stepped willingly for the first time in her life. Mimi disapproved. "These women who come to your parties — they're *courtesans*," she complained to Rose, who merely smiled and said, "Let them be whatever they want. We're eating again, aren't we? I was so tired of being poor and hungry. Weren't you?"

Mimi replied with a silent nod. They had a splendid roof over their heads, and important bankers like Gabriel Ouvrard advanced sums to help Rose along in business. There, too, Rose had determined to get ahead and be on her own. She spent her nights partying and her days following up on investment leads that were secretly passed on to her by Ouvrard. She and Mimi drove up to the stock exchange every afternoon in her black carriage with her fast-footed Hungarian horses, and in a short time, Rose had a bank account of her own. And it began to swell with profits.

One October morning Rose was enjoying a cup of coffee in her garden when Eugène came up to her with the latest broadsheet.

"You're looking like . . . such a man," she remarked. "So much like —"

"Father?" Eugène asked with a grin. He liked hearing that his fair hair and clear face bore the unique stamp of a Beauharnais. "Have a look at this," Eugène said. He handed his mother the front page of the morning's broadsheet.

Rose read the top headline aloud.

"Notice from the office of Paul Barras: As of today all unauthorized weapons will be surrendered to the office of General Bonaparte."

"Very well, Eugène," Rose said. "So, why do you have such a long face?"

"Because a commissioner just came to our door and I had to give him Father's sword."

"Why didn't you tell me someone was here?"

"There was no need, nor was there any time. The man saw the sword on the wall of our sitting room, and he demanded that we give it up. It happened just like that." He snapped his fingers, then shook his head in despair.

Rose took a small sip of coffee and patted her fat little pug, Fortuné. "How audacious!" she exclaimed. "Didn't the man know whose house this is?" She blushed in anger.

"I don't know," said Eugène, shrugging.

Rose put her coffee cup on the settee. "Oh, Eugène. I'm so sorry. I know how you adore that sword."

"It means a lot. . . . It's all we have — of him."

Rose stood up and hugged her son. "Paul's out of town, but I'll see whoever is in charge, and we shall get it back."

Eugène looked troubled. "No offense, Maman, but wouldn't it be better if I handled this?"

Rose eyed her tall, steady, earnest son. Sighing and smiling, she said softly, "You're so much older than I thought. Go ahead then, Eugène. You don't need me, do you?"

He didn't answer. Instead he left his mother and went to his room to dress.

That same afternoon Eugène entered the army headquarters at rue Capucine. Inside the main hall, an officer stopped Eugène by the door of General Bonaparte's office.

"You have business with the general?"

Eugène nodded. "I need to speak to him. It's urgent."

"What isn't?" the blue-coated guard said.

But a moment later — by the greatest of luck — he was actually on the other side of the door. And there, right before him, was the very man he was seeking. Curling his index finger as you might with a curious child, Napoleon beckoned Eugène to come forward. A wisp of a smile lay on his thin lips, but the general's cool, gray, surmising eyes never left Eugène's face.

"Well," he demanded as the tall youth drew near, "what is it?"

Eugène had prepared what he was going to say, but now his pent-up words tumbled out of his mouth in a bewildering stammer.

"My father . . . was . . ." Puzzled by what he was going to say next, Eugène stopped short. His face filled with sudden emotion and his cheeks reddened. He coughed to clear his throat.

Napoleon, amused, closed the distance between them.

"Was — what, exactly?" he asked.

"Murdered by the republic," Eugène blurted out, and he took a deep breath. He was unnerved by the general drawing so near, and though he was the taller of the two, Napoleon seemed much the larger.

Napoleon came closer still. So close, in fact, that Eugène smelled a hint of anise on his breath. Eugène glanced at the general's lips, which were slightly parted. His straight teeth were stained very black from some licorice he'd been chewing.

"You say," Napoleon whispered, "that your father was murdered by the republic. Did I hear you correctly? Is *this* what you said?"

Napoleon inched a little closer, coming so near to Eugène that the scent of licorice was overpowering, and it made Eugène's stomach growl noisily.

Napoleon smiled. "Have you eaten anything?" he asked casually. The small smile that lay upon the general's lips spread into a grin.

Eugène blinked. He found himself standing at full attention, as Napoleon seemed to circle around him.

"Stand at ease," Napoleon ordered. Then he took a small tin box out of his waistcoat pocket. "Do you like licorice?" he asked.

"When I can get it."

"Oh, you can now." Napoleon opened the tin.

Nervously, Eugène groped for a piece of candy.

"Have another," Napoleon recommended. Eugène did. His hand trembled, and he fought to steady it. Napoleon's eye missed nothing.

"Tell me now what happened to your father." The general stood, rocking on his boot heels, hands clasped behind his back. Eugène looked down at the floor. To his surprise, Napoleon's boots were caked with mud.

Then Eugène began to tell his story. "My father was a very brave man and a loyal republican. He was executed like a criminal." The words brought back a host of uncomfortable feelings. Suddenly Eugène was lost in a mist of pride, pain, and embarrassment. His lips trembled; he couldn't speak.

Napoleon regarded him with grave, luminous intensity. For a moment, neither of them said anything.

"My mother says these are trying times," Eugène said finally.

Napoleon's smile returned. "She meant to say, 'These are the times that try men's souls.' She was of course quoting Samuel Adams, one of the great patriots of the American Revolution. Is your mother much of a reader?"

Eugène sighed and relaxed for the first time. He lapsed into an uncertain smile and said, "She's a great talker."

Napoleon selected a fresh piece of licorice and popped it in his mouth. "Is she a virtuous old maid?" he asked somewhat randomly.

"My mother is a virtuous, lovely lady, sir. And if you knew her," he added, "you wouldn't cause her so much pain."

Napoleon's face showed no surprise, but perhaps some secret pleasure in this odd little interview.

"I have caused her pain?" His eyes widened with interest.

Eugène spoke now without considering the weight of his words. "Yes, you have. By confiscating Father's sword. One of your men grabbed it. It's all we have left of Father. I treasure it."

"Was he such a great man, then?"

"He was a general like yourself."

Napoleon raised his right hand, and pointed with a finger. "Do you see that pile of swords there in the corner of the room?"

Eugène acknowledged that he did.

"One of them is your father's. Go over there and find it. You are to take it home with you, and I want you to present it to your mother, with my compliments."

Eugène went swiftly to the corner of the room where the scabbards lay in a disorganized pile. He clinked through them. In a few moments he found one that was as black as jet and bore the initials A. B. in silver script. Eugène stood and walked toward the door. He was now very anxious to leave. Napoleon stood behind his teakwood desk, head bowed low, leaning awkwardly on his elbows as he wrote a letter. As Eugène opened the heavy door, Napoleon said, without taking his eyes off his paper, "Tell your mother I salute her for having so fine a son."

Twelve

Paris, 1795

Eugène came home a conquering hero, holding his father's sword high over his head as he entered the salon.

"What happened?" Rose asked in surprise.

"Well, he's just a man, after all," Eugène said as he placed the black sword back on the wall.

"Is this the same man I met the other night?" she asked. "The not-very-tall but immensely intriguing general who read my palm?"

"He said to tell you that you have a fine son," Eugène said with conspicuous pride.

"Well, I shall thank him personally for saying that, and for his kindness with regard to our sword," Rose told Eugène.

"When will you do this?"

"Tomorrow."

The following day Napoleon greeted Rose at his office door with a stiff yet cordial little bow straight from the hip. Then he turned his large eyes upon her, and she saw his evident interest.

Neither said a word. Silence filled the room. The ticking of a pendulum clock took over the absence of conversation. Another minute wore on laboriously.

They are like hot brands, those eyes, thought Rose. *Perhaps, with my shoes off, he would seem a little taller. I must remember to wear slippers when I see him again.*

"I should like to thank you for being so kind to my son." Rose spoke formally, and her eyes roved about the room so she wouldn't always have to be looking right at him.

"Well, I would be honored to come to your salon," Napoleon put in after another awkward silence.

Rose looked confused. Had she given him an invitation that she was unaware of? "But of course, General," she said softly in her slurred Caribbean lilt. "When would you like to come?"

"Tomorrow," he replied curtly. "And now, if you'll excuse me, I have an urgent letter to write."

"Of course, General," she repeated. Her voice sounded wooden to her. But there was nothing she could do about it.

After she was gone, Napoleon hunted all about his office for some sweet remnant of her scent — that perfume of lilies that was so alluring to him. For a moment he luxuriated in a brief memory of the way the widow Beauharnais had walked out of his office, as if she had all the time in the world.

The following evening Napoleon showed up at 6 rue de Chantereine at eight and was shown in by Gonthier, the heavy-browed, stoop-shouldered gardener. Napoleon observed the table decorations of hemlock sprigs and sniffed the air, which smelled of cloves. He approved of the wild game piled high upon a pine board. The place seemed festive enough, and his eye roamed the room, ferreting out more things that amused him.

Most amusing of all was Rose herself. She stood before the fire in a black muslin cape that had gold enameled lions as clasps upon the shoulders. Her long lovely arms were bare, and they glided gracefully from one task to another. Silently, he watched with glowing approval. No one he'd ever seen moved with more unconscious grace than this soft-voiced, enchanting woman.

Then his feeling of well-being changed for the worse. A sense of annoyance nettled him. The other guests, talking and eating, and enjoying the evening as much as he had been, suddenly irritated him.

Napoleon did what he always did in such situations — he acted accordingly. In this case, he tugged on Rose's elegant robe, pulling it slightly askew. Surprised, she turned. "Oh, General, it is only you."

"Only?" he countered gloomily, while at the same time glaring with open hostility at General Hoche, who stood too close to Rose, Napoleon thought.

Hoche was tall and well suited to his uniform. His rugged face bore a dueling scar like a comma between his brows. It made him appear virile and noble at the same time.

Giving no thought to Hoche's gallant good looks, Napoleon reprimanded him with a mere tilt of his chin. Immediately, Hoche looked away and, carrying off his dinner plate, disappeared into the kitchen.

"Are you sorry you did not drag your cannon in with you?" Rose asked Napoleon after Hoche was gone.

Napoleon forced a smile and said, "Perhaps you would like me better if I had?"

"Actually, I'd prefer if you didn't discipline your men at my parties."

Napoleon replied, "I like to give little lessons to whoever needs them. Especially to high-born Parisians." In reality, this was less true than he made it sound. He simply did not like tall men with raffish good looks. Moreover, he didn't fancy them when they closed him off from Rose.

"Lessons such as when you fired on the rioting people of Paris?" There was no mistaking her sharp, critical tone.

Napoleon smiled with satisfaction. "You know of my military prowess then?"

"Who doesn't?"

"Such skirmishes are only the vespers of my fame," Napoleon whispered with a sudden sweep of his hand. Then he gazed into the dancing flames of the fireplace and added, "You must have paid a lot for this wood, Madame, for it is rare indeed to have any in Paris right now." To emphasize his point, Napoleon kicked a charred log with his boot. A shower of popping sparks jumped up the flue.

"It is none of your business what I paid." Rose's eyes flashed.

Napoleon grinned. "You're most attractive when your cheeks are red," he commented, kicking the log again. Then with a few rapid steps, hands folded behind his back, he took leave of her.

/ /

"What an exasperating, bothersome little man," Rose said to Fanny a little while later. By then, most of the guests had left, but Napoleon still commanded his private corner, close to the fire. He sat on a bench-shaped chaise and read people's palms whenever they came by to pay their respects, which, to Rose's annoyance, was more often than she would've liked.

"It's the aura of fame," Fanny said with a chuckle. "Truly, he is famous. People stand and applaud him when he comes to the opera."

"And if they *didn't*, he would tell you they *did*," Rose said with uncharacteristic vehemence.

Fanny made a funny face. "I thought you two were getting along," she whispered soothingly.

Rose watched Napoleon from a safe distance. He was across the room regaling General Pichegru.

Finally, when the last of the guests had gone and only Napoleon remained, Rose went into the kitchen and was directing her staff when she felt a familiar and irksome tug on her robe.

"Madame," came Napoleon's baritone voice. "I have a proposition to make."

Rose, wishing he was out the door, said, "Does it have to do with your departure, General?"

Suddenly she felt his face pressed against hers. She smelled his lime cologne, and his fire-warmed skin was uncomfortably close. She shied away from him, but he cut her off and prevented her escape.

The cook and scullery maid pretended to have a conversation.

"Give me your hand," Napoleon told Rose.

Rose withdrew her hands, and folded her arms.

Napoleon reached out skillfully and pried her right hand away from her chest. Rose tried to appear calm; her heart was fluttering. Napoleon held her hand tightly in his. His passionate eyes seemed to swallow her whole. She felt herself reeling under his spell.

"I would like you to be my wife," Napoleon said in the most unassuming manner possible.

"Is this a joke?" Rose asked, still trying unsuccessfully to free her trapped hand.

"I speak in all earnestness," Napoleon said.

Strangely, Rose did not arch away from him this time. Instead, she relented, accepting his nearness. "I could not marry you — even if I wanted to," she said, dropping her eyes.

"Why not?" Napoleon stiffened.

"Destiny."

Napoleon's face softened. His old affable grin returned. With his free hand he poked her in the ribs with his finger.

Rose jumped. "Don't fool with me, General. I'm quite serious when I speak of destiny."

He shrugged. "So am I."

"Destiny forbids my marriage to anyone who is not a king — I mean *more* than a king."

"Which is it, then — a king or *more* than a king?"

"*More* than."

Napoleon nodded and gave her a curious smile.

"You understand my position, then," Rose said.

Napoleon grinned. "It's identical to mine. I must marry someone who is more than a queen. I have my own star of destiny to attend to, so I suppose that settles it."

"Settles *what?*"

"What we're going to do."

"Which is?"

"Whatever we want to, of course."

Thirteen

Paris, 1796

From the night of his kitchen proposal, Napoleon visited Rose every day without fail. First she tried to avoid him. But that was impossible, given Napoleon's persistence. The cunning general sniffed out her whereabouts like a hound hunting a fox. If Rose visited Thérèse Tallien, there would come a certain knock at the door: one short and two long. When Thérèse opened it, there was Napoleon, his bewitching eyes cutting through Thérèse to wherever Rose was standing or sitting in the salon.

At the theater, Napoleon waited for her at the door of the hall. It didn't matter how early or how late she was, he was always there to offer his arm. Because Napoleon was a celebrity, the gentle applause of his admirers when they were out didn't displease Rose as much as his insistent and endless advances. Once, on a drive on the Champs-Élysées, a gray horse came proudly up alongside her coach. Rose had no need to look. She knew who the rider was, who the rider would always be. There seemed to be nothing to do but wait. But what was she waiting for? She didn't know.

Napoleon's passion, both sincere and affectionate, proved greater than Rose's will to prevent it. Her strength lay in enduring impossible odds, not in rejecting tender affections. And Napoleon, for all his bizarre ways, was the most tender and forthright man she'd ever met. He was dazzlingly honest, burningly romantic. And his feelings, like those of a youth, were always on his sleeve.

One windy day in March when Rose chanced to see herself in a closely held hand mirror, she burst into tears. The corners of her eyes frightened her. She could see the beginnings of crow's feet. Middle age, wrinkles. Her heart sank. At that very moment, she gave in.

I will marry him, she thought, *and that is the end of it.*

Immediately, Rose's next concern was her children. Would they accept Napoleon as her husband? Would they accept him as their father?

That evening before she blew out the candle in Hortense's room, Rose said, "Your father's memory will never be lost. You know that, don't you?"

"I never thought it would, Maman."

Rose stroked Hortense's head the way she used to, and continued, "The Lord takes those first whom he loves the most."

Somehow, Hortense knew exactly where this was leading. "You're going to marry that strange little man, aren't you." It was not a question, the way she said it. "Well, no one will ever take Father's place, if that's what you want to know." Hortense turned away from her mother and stubbornly faced the wall. "How could you? He's too short."

"One day he may seem quite tall," Rose said as she bent down and tried to kiss Hortense, who hid her head under her blanket.

"One day we'll all be taller," Hortense said. "But not him."

"I love you very much."

Rose kissed her daughter's head again and again. Then, blowing out the candle, she went to Eugène's bedroom with the same sense of dread with which she'd entered Hortense's.

Eugène, however, being almost three years older, took the news like a soldier, sitting up against his pillows. If it wounded him at all, he gave no sign. He stared inquisitively at Rose when she sighed and said, "I need to tell you that I'm inclined to marry General Bonaparte."

Eugène didn't say anything. Then, as she prepared to present her reasoning to him, he chuckled out loud, and dismissed her with a small wave of the hand.

"Let me sleep, Maman," he murmured. Then he heaved himself down on the bed and closed his eyes.

"All right," Rose replied, feeling like a failure all over again. She snuffed out his candle. But as she stepped to the door, Eugène said into the darkness, "I'm not going to give him Father's sword."

"I don't expect you to."

"I won't give him my heart, either."

"You're not expected to."

There was an insufferable silence between them. Then Eugene commented very softly, "Maman, he *is* the best of the lot. You could do much worse."

Rose smiled. "That I know."

Another silence followed, during which Rose waited for some further comment that didn't come. At last she heard Eugène breathing deeply. He was asleep. Rose left his room and gently closed the door. *My children are wiser than I am,* she told herself. Then she let out a little halfhearted laugh. *I just hope I'm wise enough.*

Rose's friends quarreled over Napoleon, who seemed to them to be a questionable suitor, especially for her. Such a man, they said, could not love such a woman. Because of her beauty and her position in the salon society of Paris, Rose now possessed a coterie of followers and admirers. To them, she was the flower of paradise, the hummingbird.

Napoleon, on the other hand, was an audacious young general, the man who'd put down the resistance of a Paris mob by doing what no Frenchman had dared to do — firing his cannons directly into a crowd. This had put down the uprising. But it had also killed a great many innocent people. And so, for some, the general was thought to be a Corsican monster in a republican uniform.

Rose wrote down the names of her friends who were for the marriage and those who were opposed to it.

Thérèse Tallien had said, "Rose, you're too old to be picky!" And Rose knew this to be true.

Fanny had only one thing to say: "The general is a great storyteller! Isn't that enough?"

Paul Barras, for whom Rose still performed duties as a hostess, said she was a fool for not immediately accepting Bonaparte's offer. "The general is a genius you can always count on for loyalty. I leave it to you to polish his edges and make him more socially acceptable."

But Edmée told her, "He's a barbarous Corsican. How could you possibly wed such a man?"

So the opinions were as tangled as Rose's own confused feelings. Her mind was less a compass than her heart. The more her friends advised her not to marry Napoleon, the more she imagined Eliama, the prophetess, sitting like Cassandra under the tropical trees of her childhood island. "More than a queen," she heard Eliama echo in the tempest of a shell.

Paris, 1796

The following day Rose was quite surprised to receive a letter from Monsieur Ragideau, her attorney.

> *Dear Madame de Beauharnais,*
>
> *As your notary and manager of all your transactions, including those in Martinique, I feel warranted in letting you know that General Bonaparte has been to see me, and that his questions regarding your estate were most specific, and quite pointed. I shall visit you tomorrow.*
>
> *Your most humble servant,*
>
> *M. Ragideau*

Rose didn't know what to make of this. What had her adviser told Bonaparte? And what was Bonaparte doing behind her back? Why hadn't he come directly to her?

Rose was furious. In fact, angry enough to want to refuse Bonaparte's proposal of marriage. She spent an insufferable night, tossing and turning in her bed.

The next morning, exhausted from lack of sleep, Rose received yet another message. This one was from her banker, Monsieur Emmery.

Dear Madame de Beauharnais,

I have been in the presence of your suitor, Bonaparte. He has questioned me about your finances. I explained as briefly as possible that your chief holdings are tied up in the plantation in Martinique, and that your assets are somewhat uncertain.

Most faithfully,
M. Emmery

Rose read this message, and then broke down in a fit of tears. She was still crying when a knock sounded at her door. Quickly dabbing at her wet eyes with a small handkerchief, Rose stood up, went to the window, and peered out through the curtain. There was Monsieur Emmery in an amber suit, complete with pewter buttons and matching waistcoat.

Covering her surprise, Rose opened the door and let the visitor in. No sooner had Emmery taken a seat than there was another rap on the door. This time it was Monsieur Ragideau. He, too, looked elegant, all in beige and sporting a scarlet cravat.

"Come in, come in," Rose said with a forced smile. "We're having a party. I think it's a financial affair, but I'm not certain." Her eyes glanced dubiously from Ragideau to Emmery, after which she seated herself and waited for one of them to speak.

Emmery adjusted his frumpy wig. It was quite out of style, except among servants and soldiers. Perching his spectacles upon on his hooked nose, he began what sounded like a speech. "I must warn you," he said confidentially, "that your friends — and I believe I am to be counted as one — think your hasty marriage to Napoleon Bonaparte is a mistake —"

Rose interrupted, "Are you concerned because he visited you yesterday?"

Emmery mused, then gave a serious nod. "That is what is at issue, I'm afraid. Perhaps your notorious general may be something of a soldier of fortune. In any case, he thinks you are rich."

Rose threw up her hands. "Whatever would give him *that* idea?"

"Rich as a West Indian planter. Isn't that what everyone says these days?" Emmery asked.

"Not anymore," Rose said. "What did you tell him?"

"I told him the truth. What else?" He looked at Ragideau for some secret approval or support. However, Ragideau looked elsewhere on purpose. Rose caught the inference and the darting away of Ragideau's guilty eyes.

"What is your part in all of this, Monsieur Ragideau?" Rose queried. "Also, I want to hear your assessment."

Ragideau cleared his throat. "This would be . . . your

second soldier, so to say, Madame," the attorney began. "So I would ask if you are ready to marry a man who has only a sword to his name."

There came at that moment a shuffling noise in the parlor.

Ragideau said, "Rats?"

Emmery added, "Spies?"

A small gray-cloaked man stepped into the drawing room from the neighboring parlor. He took a few measured steps and then stopped. He wore an old, faded tricorn hat on his head and his cloak all but shrouded him.

"Bonaparte!" cried Rose. "How dare you lurk about in my house without my knowing it!"

"Only for your own protection, my dear Rose," he said, advancing into the carpeted salon. Napoleon looked sharply at the two advisers, who shrank a little into their chairs.

Napoleon's pale face softened into a playful smile, which was followed by a hoarse laugh.

The banker and the notary colored visibly, their faces turning toward the door, as if each — at that very same moment — wanted to go out.

"Don't worry, gentlemen," Napoleon said. "I have your interests at heart. After all, unwittingly, you've both convinced me that my beautiful Rose is a woman of means."

Ragideau raised a hand in protest. "You can still surmise this after all we've said in confidence to our client?"

Emmery, too, looked perplexed. "Yes, how can you draw such a conclusion after what we've said?"

Napoleon's easy manner and soft expression shifted rapidly. He now appeared gloomy, but the darkness faded out of his eyes, little by little, and he eased himself onto the arm of a chair, and half sat while he talked in a quiet, unassuming voice.

"Gentlemen," he spoke almost in a whisper, "if you didn't have concern for my little hummingbird here, I wouldn't have imagined that she had any money at all.

But as that is not the case, your concern shows me exactly what I already believed — that indeed Rose has a bankable dowry."

That was that. Nothing they could say or do meant a blessed thing to him. As always, Bonaparte was as decisive as he was clever. In the matter of discernment, he had no peer. He knew things. After he knew them, he sought to prove them — and then he willingly forgot them. His final judgment was an iron door that he closed forever.

So it was then that Ragideau and Emmery excused themselves and left the house. They had no wish to cross the general. Rose, on the other hand, was of a very different mind. Incensed over Napoleon's sneaky little parlor trick, she cried out, "How dare you enter my house like a spy!" Before he could say a word in his defense, she came at him again. "How dare you pry into my affairs. Why, you're just a bloodthirsty little weasel!"

Bonaparte, head bowed, hands clasped behind him, said nothing, and so she went on raging.

"How humiliating! How embarrassing! How utterly depressing! I'm so beside myself, I don't know what to do." She whirled about with her fists balled up.

"Why don't you try striking me?" Bonaparte offered. "My grandmother and my mother always did. It made them feel a lot better afterward." He smiled amiably, holding his hat in his hands.

Rose caught a glimpse of his penitent and rather pathetic face. To her surprise, Napoleon wasn't joking. On the contrary, he was quite serious.

In her anger, Rose seemed to glow with a loveliness that Napoleon secretly liked. His eyes crinkled at the sight of her being so aroused.

"You do not please me today, Bonaparte," she said after a moment of quietness. "How are we ever to marry if I cannot trust you?" Her face darkened, and she shook her head.

Bonaparte's eyes filled with humility and love. There was nothing he relished more than a lover's quarrel. Now the clever general swiftly came around the chair that stood between Rose and himself, and he dropped down on one knee.

"Normally, I don't bow — or bend," he explained. "I like to feel the world under my feet. But when I'm in the wrong, and I know it, and there is nothing to do but surrender my troops, I do so."

There he remained, on one knee, hands cupped in a prayerful position, begging forgiveness. It was overly dramatic — and she loved it.

An apology from the man who had conquered Toulon, she thought.

As Rose's temper cooled, she silently asked herself, *What do I do now?*

Bonaparte continued, "Perhaps I can offer you only my sword at this very moment; but I assure you, Josephine, if you accept my sword, you will one day rule a kingdom as large as the world."

Rose could not help herself — she burst out laughing at these lofty words. "What did you call me?"

Bonaparte sprang off the floor, and coming very

close, gave her nose a pinch. "I called you Josephine —
your new name! You are really Marie-Josèphe, are you
not? Josephine is much grander than poor drab Rose,
don't you think? Anyway, I like it better."

A moment later, the two of them were locked in a
passionate embrace.

"I cannot help myself," he whispered in her ear.
"Your kisses burn me to the bone. Look at me. I'm trembling, Josephine."

"I do not mind that name," she whispered. "It re-
minds me of my father, whom I loved so dearly."

"Josephine, Josephine," he repeated as he kissed her.

Fifteen

Paris, 1796

The following day, a courier with a letter came to Josephine's door.

My dear Josephine,

    Order your wedding dress and invite your witnesses.
    A thousand kisses,

                       Bonaparte

She picked up her own goose quill and wrote back,

My dear Bonaparte,

    I feel the haste of your departure to Italy. Why must we do everything at your speed and not mine?

                       Kisses,
                       Josephine

Whenever she felt ill at ease with something, Josephine consulted her deck of tarot cards. Hastily, she selected a card at random.

The King.

Josephine drew another card, turned it upright.

The Queen.

"How fortuitous," Mimi said. "Draw a third, Rose."

She did.

The Knave.

Smiling at Mimi, Josephine said, "Kings, queens, and commoners." She put the cards back into the deck and shuffled them three times. Then she spread them out on her marble coffee table.

"One more card, just one," Mimi advised.

The fourth card came up.

The Hanged Man.

Both women gasped. Then Josephine put the card back into the anonymity of the deck. The Hanged Man, they knew, was not death but rather mysticism, sacrifice, and self-denial. Moreover, it was the very essence of living in a world of dreams. This was neither good nor bad, but merely the condition of life. For life *was* a dream, a chaotic and crazy nightmare, most of the time. As for Bonaparte, he was all these things.

And, just like that, she vowed to marry him.

The wedding took place slowly, and then hurriedly at city hall in Paris on 9 March. Rose wore a white satin dress, and she brought Jérôme Calmelet, her family business adviser, as a witness.

Paul Barras, who had come as Bonaparte's witness, was already present when she arrived. So were Thérèse and Jean Tallien.

Barras rolled his eyes when he saw Josephine. "Bonaparte's still not here," he whispered. Then he added, by way of apology, "Our country is at war. Bonaparte is head of the army of Italy now."

Rose waited in a state of irritated silence. *Here I sit on a hard bench in a cold, wintry chamber of City Hall, awaiting a dull, cold ceremony in a room that is cheerless and unclean, and the man whom I am to marry is not even present.*

She flushed with anger just thinking about it.

What does he think he is doing? He has already pried into my financial affairs. Now he is trying to make a fool of me by not showing up for our wedding. Am I a complete fool?

Josephine's thoughts turned from herself to Hortense, who had had the good sense not to want to come. Eugène, too, had refused. Edmée would have come, so she said, but she was planning her own imminent wedding to the marquis. Besides, Bonaparte had not wanted anyone from her family, or his, to be present.

So, Tallien, all in black. Thérèse, in canary satin. The two of them looked like a couple of tropical birds. And full-faced, florid Barras in a shiny blue suit with an Attabiah silk scarf, looking pleased with himself, as always.

Monsieur Calmelet, who didn't know the others very well, seemed a little out of place in his formal banker's frock coat, but he readily offered a smile whenever anyone smiled at him.

"You look darling," Thérèse whispered to Rose, and she gave her a peck on the cheek.

"Do you think I look old? I *feel* old."

Thérèse shook her head and chuckled.

"Come now," she coaxed. "We must be patient with these important men of ours. Say, doesn't Tallien look glorious? He does, doesn't he? But he's pacing back and forth — and it's not even *his* wedding. I wish he'd stop that, but he won't, so there's the end of my fussing over it."

"*What* wedding?" Rose said, raising her voice so everyone could hear her.

At the same time, the tired notary at the wooden table covered with stale old books and crumbs of long-forgotten meals got to his feet. Mumbling to himself, he built a small fire in the fireplace. Soon the disheveled little room was scented with warm, crackling pine.

Rose angrily fidgeted with her tricolor sash, a gift from Bonaparte. The long minutes and then the longer hours went by. The notary's pince-nez fell off his nose, and his head dropped forward. He was sound asleep. Then his head went down, striking the desk. Suddenly, the awakened man climbed awkwardly out of his high-backed chair and excused himself.

"Where are you going in such a hurry?" Rose asked.

"Home," he replied. Throwing a dark cloak over his shoulders, he added, "See you don't burn the place down."

Rose ran after him, her white gown whispering silkily as she went out into the cold empty hall.

"But who will conduct the ceremony?" she cried as the strange bony man vanished into the shadows.

"My intern," he shot back. "He's *had* dinner."

Rose felt like sobbing. Instead she fought back the tears. Then, reluctantly, she returned to the notary's nasty little office.

Another hour passed. At last, a well-dressed boy appeared in the doorway, rubbing his wind-chilled hands. His cheeks were red.

Paul Barras snorted in his sleep, his legs stretched out before the fire. The untrimmed candlewick curled until it looked exactly like Barras's nose. The fire in the fireplace smoldered. An hour dragged by, and part of another. The night was hopeless and sad.

Then, all at once, in a flurry of excitement, Napoleon burst into the chamber with the March night still clinging to his royal purple robe. Underneath he wore an impeccable white and blue uniform. He was cleaner and more scrubbed than Rose had ever seen him. Moreover, his bedeviled eyes gleamed with boyish good humor.

Bonaparte exclaimed, "All right, let's get to it." At once his magic spell was cast into the dead air of the dozing chamber. Everyone shuffled into their proper positions.

The notary boy asked questions, and with a flourish filled out the marriage license in his best script. When he came to the part about where Rose was from, and whether she had a birth certificate, she paled.

"I haven't one," she confessed.

Those gathered in the dimly lighted room stared in surprise.

"Well," she added apologetically, "it's on account of the British taking over the Windward Islands. Our papers all went up in smoke."

The notary boy pursed his lips and touched his quill feather to them. "I see. And you, sir?" he asked Bonaparte respectfully.

"Here," Bonaparte answered. He tossed a heavy paper onto the table.

The intern examined it up and down.

"Is the ink still wet?" Bonaparte joked. He felt foolish, as the certificate was really his brother Joseph's. By borrowing it, he'd advanced his age two years, making him twenty-eight, not twenty-six.

The document, however, was written in Italian, and it was obvious to Bonaparte that this young man had no idea what it said.

Napoleon laughed. "Of course it's forged — like everything else in Paris." This got a guffaw from Paul Barras.

At last, the notary boy said, "Napoleon Bonaparte, born in Ajaccio on 5 February, 1768. Correct, sir?"

Bonaparte nodded obligingly.

Josephine said, "Mine will read Marie-Josèphe Rose Beauharnais, born in Martinique on 23 June, 1767."

Dutifully, the intern wrote this down on the license. Then he read it aloud, and asked if it was correctly done.

Rose agreed that it was.

Like Napoleon, Rose had lied about her age. Because she had no birth certificate, she'd been able to create a fictitious age, and made herself younger by four years. This suited her well, as she wished to be closer in age to her husband who, in fact, wanted to be older. However, neither knew the lie of the other, so it didn't matter.

Finally the desperately unromantic and somewhat confusing wedding of Napoleon Bonaparte and Rose de Beauharnais was over and done with — much to their relief.

The newlyweds then went home to celebrate, and were alone at last, except for the dog Fortuné, who'd waited up for them.

Two days later, Napoleon left for Nice to review his soldiers, who would soon be marching to Italy to engage in the war that would change the fortunes of France and the lives of the newly married Bonapartes.

Italy, 1796

As a twenty-six-year-old commander of the troops on the Italian front, Napoleon Bonaparte had to prove himself to his generals and to his men. Italy was an important front to the French. It was constantly being attacked by Austria. Therefore, Napoleon's presence was pivotal. He needed to drive back the Austrian army and, if he could, conquer all of Italy for France. The rest of Europe awaited him — but only if he could manage to grab up Italy first.

Napoleon had more confidence in himself than anyone else did, except Paul Barras, who by this time was one of the leaders of the Directory that ran France. It was Barras who had ordered Bonaparte to Italy. However, Napoleon's first command proved to be a challenge. The well-seasoned generals towered over the untried and shoddy man who moved among them in a dirty gray greatcoat. He looked diminutive in the shadows of these experienced military men, and at first they tried to intimidate him with their stature. But whether they were standing or seated, Napoleon found a clever way to reverse the position of their power. When the generals were on their feet, Napoleon reclined in a chair. When they were seated, he stood over them. All in all he was always one step ahead of anyone who tried to outsmart him.

The army that Bonaparte commanded was another story. As he reviewed the troops, Bonaparte saw a dispirited, poorly paid, ill-equipped bunch of soldiers who had no will to do much of anything.

Napoleon went before the irresolute columns of threadbare men leaning on their carbines and let them get a good look at him.

Seeing Bonaparte's stature, many of the soldiers laughed. Yet Napoleon walked with dignity before them and he spoke like a prince, a poet, and a theatrical performer. No one expected this. The ragged, half-starved soldiers stood up straight and listened.

Bonaparte eyed them defiantly. Half smiling, he said, "For the brave, there will always be food in my army. But the cowardly will feed themselves to the crows. I will see to that myself."

Every face was glued to Napoleon. No one moved. Everyone listened, and there was a tension in the air as he spoke with a biblical passion.

"Though you are nearly naked," he said, "you shall be clothed. Though weakened, you shall grow strong. Though no glory falls upon you, I will lead you into the fertile plains of the earth. Cities of silver and gold shall fall into your dominion. And you shall have honor and power, and you shall grow fat from the food I put before you. I will lead you on the paths of righteous victory. There is but one question I shall ask . . . one question, that is all."

The soldiers straightened up even more. What was

the question? They waited for it, and Napoleon made them wait even longer as he paced back and forth like a tireless panther.

Finally, he shouted, "The question is, Who will follow me to glory?"

The stunned men cheered. Someone yelled, "Long live Bonaparte!" A great loud chant rose up in the well-defined ranks, and Bonaparte's name rang out like music. *Bona-parte, Bona-parte!* The ragged soldiers kept up this throbbing, ecstatic rhythm long after Napoleon left the field. And the generals heard the chant.

There was no insincerity in Bonaparte's words. He meant everything he said. The stunning effect of his speech, his demeanor, and his plan of action was enough to give his men more guts than gunpowder. But that was really all they needed to send the Austrian enemy running out of Italy. The French, anyway, won the first skirmishes under Bonaparte's command. Afterward, he gathered up his enemy's fallen flags and had them couriered to Barras in Paris. Barras, knowing their worth as propaganda, took care of the rest, and in no time the broadsheets were full of Bonaparte's bluster and bravery.

Josephine noticed a change as well. When she went to the theater, people applauded her entrance more loudly than the actors' curtain calls. Wherever she went, in fact — salons, balls, cafés — Josephine was noticed, recognized, and met with enthusiastic cheers. Meanwhile, her husband's letters arrived daily. Her sudden fame and Napoleon's weekly raft of letters were overwhelming, and Josephine complained to Thérèse, "Bonaparte is mad for me. I am drowning in his mail."

"We all should be treated so uncivilly," Thérèse mocked. "Isn't this what you wanted?"

Josephine wasn't so sure.

Always letters to answer, always letters to read — letters, letters, letters. So many fluttering about the house, she felt a loss of breath, as if the words themselves were spies out to trap her soul and pin it to the page. Bonaparte went on unchecked. His pen, like his cannon, never stopped. Without his knowledge, he was bombarding her.

One day the most passionate of all letters arrived and Josephine felt nettles just reading it.

To live for Josephine is the history of my life! I am working to return to you, I am dying to approach you! Fool that I am, I see not that I am more and more drifting away from you! How much space, how many mountains separate us! How long before you can read these words, the feeble expression of a throbbing soul in which you rule! Ah, my adored wife, I know not what future awaits me, but if it keeps me much longer away from you, it will be intolerable, my courage reaches not that far.

Reading this was almost an effort for Josephine. *Is my husband really this romantic? I am still somewhat unsure of how I feel about him, and this troubles me more than I can ever say.*

Her letters — far fewer than his — were short and subdued. Bonaparte complained bitterly, *Your last letter is cold, like your friendship. I have not found in it the fire that glows in your eyes, the fire that I have imagined at least to be there.*

While his letters raged of love and sorrow, Bonaparte pressed his army deeper into Italy, and each of his subsequent conquests became the gossip of Paris. He was a lion, an eagle, people said. Inspired by these words of praise that he read in the broadsheets, Napoleon drew an insignia — a fleur-de-lys with bees over it and on top of them an eagle, symbol of the republic.

"The bees are from an ancient Corsican seal that comes from my family," Bonaparte proudly told his aide Murat. "One day, I expect to see them engraved on every lamppost in France." He smiled inwardly as his vision carried him into the future, where his wealth and influence would command the entire nation.

As the days went by, more and more carts returned

to Paris loaded with Napoleon's looted treasure. Although he'd forbidden such behavior in his soldiers, he himself pillaged from Italian museums, homes, and castles. A fortune in plunder poured into France, and the word spread that the little general was making the country rich again.

At the same time, he found himself consumed with jealousy. One day as his suspicions raged he dispatched General Murat to Paris to find out why Josephine was not writing to him. The same day on the Italian front, the painted porcelain miniature of Josephine that Bonaparte wore around his neck broke into pieces and fell tinkling to his feet. Shocked, Napoleon told his aide-de-camp to remove the ribbon from around his neck.

"What do you think this means?" he asked.

The aide's hooded eyes revealed nothing.

"It means," Bonaparte decided, "that my wife is ill."

Seventeen

Paris, 1796

When Murat returned to the front without Josephine, Bonaparte ordered aide after aide to fetch her from Paris to Italy. Each time Josephine refused to join him. And each time he said, "I cannot go on without her." He dictated a letter to his secretary, and it took him forever to formulate his words. He kept starting and stopping, turning and grinding his heels in the grass. By the time the secretary put down the last syllable of ink, the shadows of the orange trees had darkened the table and the day was nearly done.

15 June, 1796

To Josephine: My life is a ceaseless Alpine burden. An oppressive foreboding prevents me from breathing. I live no more, I have lost more than life, more than happiness, more than rest! I am without hope. I send you a courier. He will remain only four hours in Paris, and return with your answer. Write me only ten lines; they will be some comfort to me. . . . Forgive me, my beloved. The passion you have inspired in me has taken my reason away; I cannot find it again. One is never cured of this evil. My contemplations are so horrible, that it would be a satisfaction to see you; to press you for two hours to my heart, and then, to die together!

. . . I have always been fortunate. Never has Fate stood against my wishes, and today it strikes me where only wounds are possible. Josephine, how can you delay so long in writing me? Your last laconic note is dated the 3rd of this month, and this adds to my sorrow. Yet I have it always in my pocket. Your portrait and your letters are always under my eyes.

I am nothing without you. I can scarcely understand how I have lived without knowing you.

. . . A thousand kisses on your eyes and lips! . . .

adored wife, how mighty is your spell . . . I have a burning fever. Retain the courier no longer than six hours; then let him return, that he may bring me a letter from my sovereign.

N. B.

Eighteen

Paris to Milan, Italy, 1796

Josephine opened the door at 6 rue de Chantereine. In front of her was a man who looked exactly like her husband. Was she dreaming? She wanted to pinch herself, but the man, seeing her confusion, smiled and said, "No, I am not Napoleon — don't you recognize me?" Then Josephine realized her mistake. She wasn't dreaming, she was awake, and this was Napoleon's brother Joseph standing in her doorway.

"My brother wants you with him, and this time he won't take no for an answer," Joseph explained.

"Please, come in," Josephine said wearily. She'd been through this before, and would probably go through it again if she didn't acquiesce. Outside the gate Joseph's black carriage drawn by two sturdy white Hanoverians awaited his return. Glancing at it, she saw Napoleon's aide, Junot, wave from within. *So, he sent two strong-arms this time,* she thought.

"Are you ready to go?" Joseph inquired, shifting his feet moodily in the entryway.

"I've been ready for days," Josephine lied as she fanned herself and squinted in the bright sunlight coming in the open door. "Tell me, Joseph, is it unbearably hot in Milan?"

"As hot as it is dusty," he answered. "Why are you smiling?" Joseph moved his jaw from left to right, a nervous mannerism he'd adopted from his brother.

"Oh, you do so resemble him," she commented. "For a moment —"

"You wouldn't say that if you'd seen him a few days ago." Joseph, still leaning in the open doorway, looked down the sumptuous hall. Greek and Roman statuettes decorated white ionic pedestals, and there were Italian portraits on the walls and potted palms on either side of the door. "I can see why you don't want to leave," he murmured. "This place is beautiful — even more lovely than when I saw it last."

Josephine raised her fan and blushed. "Heavens, I've not asked you in. Forgive me, *mon frère*."

Stepping into the cool, polished hall, Joseph remarked, "Pretty as this is, my brother's headquarters, the Serbollini Palace, will suit you even better. Did you know he was waiting for you there?"

Josephine sat beside Joseph on a silk chaise. Seating himself with the grateful sigh of a much older, heavier man, Joseph took off his blue tricorn and sought to tidy his thinning hair. He was a man very much concerned with appearances, especially his own. He had a deceptive calm that Josephine didn't trust. Why should she? She knew Napoleon's family talked about her behind her back. Worse, their gossip was designed to cause harm. Why? Simply because they thought their brother was married to a woman with a name and no money. She had holdings — but who didn't? She had no liquid currency, no assets that could be converted into immediate capital. And this, more than anything else, troubled the greedy, grasping Bonapartes.

Now Josephine watched Joseph as his eyes roved critically about the room, taking in every piece of art that she'd recently purchased and, most likely, evaluating its worth so that he could report this on the sly to Napoleon.

She watched him, and thought to herself, *Oh, these sneaky Bonapartes, they'll get you any way they can. The Clan is what I call them. A petty snake's nest of brothers, sisters, and that one great imperial and poisonous mother. I know they're all gathered together in Milan, waiting to hiss in my face. What am I to do?*

In the end, Josephine decided she had no choice but to leave Paris and go to Milan as Napoleon wanted. She might not have gone at all but he'd threatened her with consequences. If she didn't leave with Joseph and Junot, he promised, he would abandon his post just as the Austrians were waging a grand counterattack against France.

If I don't go, I'm a double traitor — to Bonaparte and to my country.

So she departed 6 rue de Chantereine full of misgivings. With a tearful face she clutched Fortuné, for whom she had bought a brand-new collar, and said good-bye to Mimi and her children.

Soon afterward, the procession of three carriages left the city. Josephine traveled in one with Joseph, Junot, and his aide-de-camp, young Hippolyte Charles. Behind the first carriage was a second carrying Josephine's maid, plus two additional servants and Fortuné, whose bad habit of biting people tended to isolate him on trips. In the third carriage was none other than the Duke of Serbollini, whose palace was to be Josephine's new home.

So the train of coaches went forth, and the horses' hooves echoed off the stone-fronted houses of Paris for the last time.

Two weeks later, they arrived in Milan.

*   *   *

Despite the delays and discomforts, Josephine met her husband with tender vows, and as soon as he sequestered her in a private section of the palace, she broke down and wept. The carriage dust veiled her clothes and a headache pounded in her temples. Truth be known, Josephine hated traveling more than anything. Her only outlet for her recent suffering was tears. After drying her eyes, however, she allowed herself to be overwhelmed by the luxury of the palace. Venetian mirrors glittered in their gilded frames, and the splendor of marble columns and finely embossed wallpaper was charming beyond belief.

All the while, Bonaparte stood back, rocking on his heels and smiling with great satisfaction. His lips trembled when he asked, "But is it good enough for you, *ma petite fleur?*"

Josephine let out a delicious little laugh, and her mouth turned up at the corners. "This is fit for a Bourbon queen," she cried. "I don't know what's the matter with me. Why didn't I come sooner?"

To Josephine, Napoleon seemed a different man —

in appearance especially. There he was at Serbollini, clean, soft-voiced. There she was, tired and dusty, seated on a vast divan of tangerine-colored Chinese silk. Her fingers touched the surface as if they were tripping on water. Bonaparte sat close to her.

"What is that you smell of?" she inquired. "Oranges?"

Napoleon chuckled. "Do you like it?"

She nodded. "Very much."

"Joseph gave this scent to me the day he married Julie Clary. I bathed in it for you this morning." His gray eyes glimmered. "A thousand years ago, it was . . ."

The dog days of summer followed one after another. However, Napoleon and Josephine lived for the cool Milanese nights in the glittering Serbollini Palace. She loved to dress like a queen, and to act like one, too. But she soon grew tired of the parties, the small talk, the family quarrels, the ubiquitous Bonapartes coming and going with the self-importance of royalty.

"I am so fed up with Napoleon's family," Josephine

complained to her maid one afternoon as she took a cool bath in water scented with rose petals.

"Don't you like that handsome devil Lucien?" the girl asked.

Josephine made a face. "I trust him about as much as an adder."

"But he's so elegant and good-looking."

Josephine wore a white muslin dress for lunch and an ivy wreath in her hair. Afterward, she took her coffee in the garden with Fortuné at her side. Meanwhile. Bonaparte chatted idly with his mother, Madame Letizia, whose disapproving eye never lost sight of Josephine and her small dog. Letizia hated her daughter-in-law, and was convinced that with the help of her family, she could promote a divorce.

Josephine, for her part, found it best to ignore the Bonapartes. She wrote to Thérèse,

If fate would bring me good health, then I should be entirely happy. I possess the most amiable husband that

can be found. I have no occasion to desire anything; my wishes are his. The whole day he is worshipping me as if I were a deity; it is impossible to find a better husband. He writes often to my children — he loves them very much. He sent Hortense a beautiful enameled watch ornamented with fine pearls. He sent Eugène a fine gold watch, too.

But before she finished her letter, a single tear wandered down her cheek.

"What is it?" her maid whispered. "You were so happy."

"I'm sad again."

"But why?"

"I may never have children again."

"Don't *ever* say that. It's bad luck."

Josephine shook her head and wiped away her tears. "My only luck was to be born under a star of destiny. Thus, my fate and my husband's are one and the same.

There's nothing we can do except live out our lives for better or worse."

Josephine looked despondently at her sandaled feet. She went on talking. "I overheard him say, when he was asked who was the best woman at the table, 'The one who bears the most children.' He didn't think I heard that, but I did."

"Another of his crude jokes," the maid said gently.

Josephine looked northward toward the dry hills and vineyards. Then she bit a small hangnail off her first finger. "I fear I'll never bear him an heir," she sighed.

Nineteen

Milan, 1796

What was left of the summer dwindled away. Some golden days, some silver nights. Some good times, some bad. But mostly good. For the first time, Josephine felt that she might really be in love with Napoleon Bonaparte. She was a woman of many moods, just as he was a man of great moodiness. But now their mood of love melted into one stream and flowed through both of their hearts.

However, the days of quietude were soon over. The war with Austria was not finished, and Bonaparte traveled to Brescia to set up his new headquarters.

A few days later, Bonaparte wrote that he could not wage war without her. He asked, then *demanded*, that

Josephine come to Brescia immediately. No mention was made of the dangers of traveling the roads of battle.

Reading this, Josephine acted on a hot impulse. She set forth by carriage the next morning with her maid and one of Bonaparte's aides-de-camp. On the way from Milan to Brescia, they encountered miles of marching soldiers. Columns of smoke rose from the wheat-planted plain across the vineyard road. Cannons grumbled in the far distance, sounding as much like summer thunder as the weapons of warfare.

Napoleon's aide reassured the two women that they were safe in his care. But they remained uncertain until they arrived in Brescia late that afternoon.

Bonaparte was so happy to see her, he fell to his knees and clasped Josephine's waist. A crowd of well wishers, Italians from the town, applauded as the two embraced. Then, without wasting any time, Napoleon took her to a small villa where he had her all to himself.

"You look thin, Bonaparte," she said disparagingly. It was true — he looked quite wan and woebegone, and his clothes were stained and tattered.

"But you look wonderful," Napoleon said. For the next few hours, despite the long hot journey, he hugged and caressed her. But she didn't complain. *How can I?* she thought. *After all, I am the wife of a great general. I must share his hardships, and his frivolities, his insolent teasing and pinching, as well as his odd letters.*

For a day they sequestered themselves in the little villa surrounded by mulberry trees and windblown poplars. Then, while they were having a lunch of black olives, peppered oil, good bread, and dark Tuscan wine, Bonaparte's aide interrupted their lunch to say that the Austrian general Wurmser was on the outskirts of the village. At once they — Napoleon and Josephine — left for Verona, but no sooner did they arrive than the troops of Austria attacked the town. Bonaparte then took Josephine to Castel Nuovo, not far from Verona, Italy.

On the way, for the first time, Josephine saw the

dead and the dying. She saw the wounded, who crept along the roadside. This was more than she could bear. She broke down. "Murder and massacre," she said, weeping, "that's all this war is. You say you're conquering new territory for the good of France. But I say you're fighting Austria for one reason only — to defeat them."

"There is more to it than that," Bonaparte said mildly. "It's not about enemies, it's about Italy. If we can win all of Italy, our borders will again be safe. As it is now the Austrians want to do the same thing — grab Italy for themselves to protect their borders. You see, war is sublime as well as tragic. Glorious as well as awful. But there's no use talking about it, *ma chérie*."

Seeing Josephine so saddened, Napoleon smothered her with kisses and then promptly got out of the carriage. His hand clasped the open window frame.

"I will see you in Milan after I've made Wurmser pay for making my beloved cry."

"No, no, Bonaparte," Josephine cried. "You don't understand me at all."

Bonaparte's face was drawn. Opening the carriage door, he asked gently, "What would you have me do?"

Josephine shook her head, wiped her eyes of tears, but said nothing.

"Perhaps I should not leave you," Napoleon said. Patiently he awaited her response.

"Do whatever you must do," Josephine told him. "I'm sorry I cry so much. Just promise me that you won't stay here."

"Why not? Have you some premonition?"

"Some evil will happen if you stay. I'm certain of it."

They both listened as the cannons thundered in the wheat fields beyond the mulberry wood. A hawk's wheedling cry was heard as it dropped low and disappeared into a stand of poplars. There was a moment of stillness during which the snorting of the carriage horses was the dominant sound. Then came some big fat drops of rain that fell like lead on the dusty road. Little puffs of white smoke lifted up where the raindrops struck.

"You surely are my star of fortune," Bonaparte said. He rested his forearms on Josephine's lap and looked into her eyes. "I could stay here forever," he murmured.

"Where?"

"In your sight. Always."

"Why?"

"Because it's the place where men lose their souls, and I have no need of mine now that I have yours."

The rain came hard as he finished speaking.

"You must go," he said. "I must as well. If your intuition is right, Wurmser is very near." He then addressed his aide and told him to go straight to Peschiera on the banks of Lake Gorda. "I'll send another aide to bring you to Castiglione," he told Josephine. "You'll be safe there, for the moment. There's no sense in trying to go to Milan yet. Now I must see if I can hurt Wurmser in return for making you cry."

Josephine and her company went on in the direction of Lake Gorda, which they reached by that evening. Through the interlaced pine trees by the lake, Josephine recognized the Austrian fires as they flickered near the shore.

Then, at last, late in the evening, the carriage rumbled up to the little town of Peschiera.

A soldier then escorted the women to a small country inn made of black quarry stone, and after a wonderful meal of roasted wildfowl and wine, Josephine and her maid retired to a darkly lit room where they spent a wakeful night listening to the intermittent crackling of faraway guns.

Early in the morning, Bonaparte's second aide appeared with a fresh escort of cavalrymen. Finishing a hasty breakfast, the women departed amidst myriad noises — the creaking of leather and the clanking of steel and the muffled clumping of the mounted men who flanked the carriage on either side. They went on, and soon the woods were popping with musket fire. In the sunlit spaces between the pines, Josephine saw plumes of powder and sometimes spied a jet of flame. The carriage plunged onward, swaying left and right, bucking along the badly pocked road.

Her maid constantly wrung her hands. The tension was almost more than she could handle. Josephine showed signs of fatigue and fear, but she masked them as best she could. She was at heart a very good mimic when she needed to be. In this case, she pretended to be a soldier.

The coach rocked along the high-crowned, potholed road, and the leather braces strained and the bouncing wheels seemed about to come off. Far out in the lake an Austrian gunboat fired a hail of grapeshot that clattered in the tops of the trees. Branches fell and struck the coach. One load of grapeshot, a small cluster of cast-iron balls, found its mark. A horse soldier buckled, then toppled off his mount. At once the carriage ground to a halt and the dust rose up around it.

"Everyone out," the aide ordered.

Another spray of grapeshot plowed the upper levels

of the pines. Branches sailed down lazily and tangled among others in their descent.

"Hurry, get into that ditch," the aide said.

Josephine and her maid followed his instructions.

"Stay down so the sharpshooters can't see you, and keep moving forward on your hands and knees. We're going back for that fallen soldier. We'll meet you up ahead."

"How shall we creep along with these heavy skirts of ours?" the girl asked in a shrill voice.

"Like children do," Josephine replied, and she hitched up her petticoated dress and carried it trussed over her right arm. Crouching low, she ran quickly and her maid followed suit. Over their heads, bullets rattled and kicked up some dirt. Once, Josephine was stung on the arm by a flying chip of stone. She said nothing, though, and kept her pace with her dress hitched high and her head held low.

After a good while, the coach caught up with them, and by then, they were out of range of the Austrian sharpshooters. In the nearby town of Deserzano, the carriage and horses were given water. Josephine and her companions drank red wine out of leather wineskins and ate dry corncakes wrapped in cornhusks. The battle of the night before was still going on, and Josephine looked with great pity on the fallen horses in the fields of ripening grain. The blue summer sky was smeared with smoke. The wooden hospital carts wobbled as they were pushed through the orchards of burned-out olive trees. The air smelled of carrion.

"Bonaparte says war is sublime," Josephine told her maid in disbelief.

"All men think so," the girl returned. Her hair was plastered to her face, and bits of yellow straw stuck to her cheeks.

"What are we to do with men who love honor as well as horror?" Josephine asked. In the field across the way she watched the crows descend on the nameless dead.

Twenty

Milan, 1796

Safe at last in the fortress of Serbollini, Josephine resumed the social duties of a general's wife. The summer season had swelled and subsided. Autumn came. The grapes grew, the grains ripened. The apples of autumn reddened and were harvested. Josephine wrote letter after letter to her husband, but Bonaparte, who seemed to enjoy the role of the suffering spouse, complained to her, as he always did, that she never wrote enough.

One night Josephine went to the city of Genoa to celebrate her husband's triumph over the Austrian army. At the gaudy reception where she was the guest of honor, Josephine pretended to feel as glamorous as she looked.

However, that same night, Bonaparte, unable to be

away from Josephine any longer, rode home to Milan. His letter telling her this, in advance, was delayed. Josephine knew nothing of it. She had journeyed to a festivity in his honor while he burst into the Serbollini Palace only to find her gone. This reduced Napoleon to a fit of rage. He lay down in their bedroom, murmuring dark oaths. He clutched at a slipper of Josephine's and wept over it as he rubbed it against his unshaven cheek. Soon his body's gyrations turned violent. Servants, hearing him thrash around on the floor, begged to know if they could help him.

Finally, he pulled himself together and penned a letter to Josephine that released the demons from his heart.

Milan, 27 November, 1796

I have just arrived in Milan and rushed to our apartments. I have left everything to see you, to press you in my arms; . . . you are not there! You are pursuing a circle of festivities through the cities. You go away from me at my approach; you trouble yourself no more about your dear Napoleon. A spleen has made you love him; inconstancy renders you indifferent.

Accustomed to dangers, I know a remedy against ennui and the troubles of life. The wretchedness I endure is not to be measured; I am entitled not to expect it.

I will wait here. . . . Do not trouble yourself. Pursue your pleasures; happiness is made for you. The whole world is too happy when it can please you, and your husband alone is very, very unhappy.

Stony faced, Napoleon delivered this vitriolic letter to a courier. But his cry of anguish did not reach Josephine because the courier was delayed.

Bonaparte, finding no message from Josephine by return courier, dropped into a state of complete despondency. He wrote,

Farewell, adorable wife! . . . May fate pour into my heart every trouble and every sorrow; but may it

send to my Josephine serene and happy days! Who deserves it more than she? When it is well understood that she loves me no more, I will garner up into my heart my deep anguish, and be content to be in many things at least useful and good to her.

The sadness he felt was like a chasm inside him. He lay in his bed, with his long cotton nightcap on, thinking that he would take a mistress and be done with husband-and-wife remorse.

Napoleon feared to know what he already suspected of Josephine. Unable to sleep, he got up, lighted a candle, and wrote letters while the small white owls hunted in the moonlight and the tame Serbollini doves pecked at the glass to be let in.

Milan, 1797

By the beginning of 1797, Napoleon had established that he was a force to be reckoned with by any and all European powers. And, in a sense, he was remaking the maps of Europe. Not only was Italy under his control but he had captured part of Switzerland and the west bank of the Rhine. England was now only a whisper away from Napoleon's sword.

In April 1797 Bonaparte strolled into the Austrian court at Leoben, and charmed and maddened whomever he met. Without hesitation, deals were rendered and treaties were signed, so that when he returned to the Serbollini Palace, the city of Milan and the region of Lombardy welcomed him with open arms not only as a hero of war but a giver of peace. He was the champion of France and now of Italy. The treaty with Austria brought peace to a region that had been at war for years.

Josephine, in her own soothing way, healed Bonaparte's jealous heart. She eased his longing to hold her in his arms by letting him, and so he held her — for hours at a time. To the people of Italy, Josephine had become as much of an icon as Napoleon. They loved her and treated her like a queen. She was a dignified and lovely woman who personified all that was good and true to the Italian people. Under Napoleon and Josephine's watchful eyes, the Italians felt their peace was secure. It was a time of celebration, a return to long-ago days when monarchs were considered the benevolent parents of the countries they ruled. And although the Bonapartes were not exactly rulers, they were imagined to be.

"Your son may look a little different to you," Napoleon warned Josephine on the day they showed up at his newly appointed summer castle, Villa Crivelli at

Mombello, about ten miles from Milan. Eugène was coming to visit that same day, and Josephine was excited and glad. This annoyed Napoleon, if only because it drew attention away from him. Moreover, he was very proud of the splendid outdoor piazza, and he wanted her to see everything through his own affectionate and doting eye.

The place after all was a present to her: a paradise of gardens and swans, olive trees, wind-swayed poplars, and wall-hugging honeysuckle that drenched the air with its cloying smell. The Villa Crivelli, as it was known, had the charmed air of a medieval court surrounded by birds, beasts, and flowers.

Bonaparte could not contain his pleasure. Dancing about, he pinched his wife's cheek. "I love it when you're expectant," he said. "I just want you to always be expectant — with me."

"Why do you think Eugène will look different?" Josephine inquired, rubbing her bruised cheek.

"You'll see soon enough, *mon amour*. I summoned him from Paris the moment I knew we'd have this villa to ourselves. I want it to be perfect — for you."

The estate was charming to Josephine, but nothing about it was lovelier than the thought of seeing her son after so many months of separation.

Later that day, in the trellised garden, over which a roof of passionflowers had grown in a profuse tangle, Josephine sipped mint tea and waited for her son's arrival. In a myrtle grove nearby, an orchestra called upon by Napoleon to play military tunes sawed away at their strings. *Their music doesn't rival the songbirds of these Lombardy meadows*, Josephine thought. Still, she told Napoleon they did.

Eugène rode up at dusk in the uniform of a horse soldier, a hussar. When she first saw him coming up the road, Josephine drew a deep breath. *Is this really Eugène?*

For she saw a man, not a boy — a man who wore a saber and sat upon a horse as proudly as any cavalryman.

As he drew near, Josephine heard his scabbard rattle, and she watched in stunned silence as he dismounted slowly and took off his tall black-and-red-plumed hat.

Again she asked herself, *Is this truly my son?*

The man was only a few yards away now. He wore a well-fitted blue jacket with a cape of fringed silk that hung decoratively off his right shoulder. Angled across his chest was a wide black military belt.

The face — that's what troubles me most — is bearded!

She rushed forward to embrace him, expecting to feel the rough bristle of whiskers. But when her soft cheek touched his, she felt wet and greasy. Her face came away blackened.

"Heavens, what is this, Eugène?" Josephine cried as she daubed her cheeks with a white handkerchief.

Eugène gave his mother a sheepish grin. "All the young officers wear it, Maman."

"What is it?" she laughed, hugging and kissing him again.

Eugène rubbed his chin and looked at his blackened hand.

"It's just black wax," he said. "On the battlefield, it looks like a beard. Very convincing."

"Convincing of *what?*"

"Age, Maman. Maturity."

Josephine shook her head and sucked air through her teeth. "There's time for that," she said, shaking her head, her eyes moist with emotion. Then she added, "Besides, your beard should be the color of wheat, not this ghastly shade of black."

"I'll have it off straightway, Maman. No need for it while I'm here on vacation. How do you like the uniform?"

"It's wonderfully becoming."

Eugène responded with a minor shoulder adjustment of his cape, after which he shook the dust off it with a flourish, smiled, and said, "The general has made me second lieutenant in the first regiment of hussars."

"How impressive!" Josephine was really quite awed by this as well as her grown-up son with his broad shoulders and regal stance.

"That isn't all," Eugène said eagerly. "I'm also adjutant of the commanding general of the Army of Italy. How do you like that?"

Josephine cocked an eyebrow. "Is that *all?*" she asked, with a teasing glance.

"No, Maman, there's more." Beaming, he walked in a small circle, hands behind his back.

"What could *possibly* be added to such glory?" Josephine asked.

"He intends . . . the general does . . . to take me with him to —"

Then he stopped short, wondering if he ought to continue. From the balcony above, he saw Napoleon give a small wave. This had the effect of humbling him into silence.

"*Which* general, Eugène?" Josephine asked.

"*The* general," he answered.

"And where does he think he is taking you . . . *the* general?"

The tall boy in the hussar uniform tossed a quick look toward the balcony. Bonaparte was gone. Eugène leaned closer to his mother and spoke in a cautious whisper. "Egypt," he said, his voice dropping low.

Josephine felt a tremble pass through her body.

Being with Eugène made Josephine all the more lonely for Hortense, who was at a boarding school in Paris. She also longed to be among her Paris friends — Fanny, Paul Barras, Thérèse, Edmée, and all the rest. Instead of a warm reunion, Josephine found herself in the midst of a Bonapartian gathering. Napoleon's mother, Madame Letizia, suddenly appeared with Napoleon's brothers and sisters, which made Josephine nervous and ill at ease. Napoleon, though, was overjoyed. His dream had always been to preside over a military headquarters that was also an aristocratic home. He desired a royal court, over which he was the benign lord. At Villa

Crivelli tents canopied the gardens and all military business was conducted outdoors while the family raged and frolicked within. Josephine was miserable.

As the summer came to a close, Josephine found herself dreaming of Paris and wishing all of her in-laws would go away. Napoleon buried himself in his work and spent less time with Josephine than he would have liked. But then, he had so little time that wasn't already taken by brothers and sisters and most of all, his mother. Fortunately, by the end of July, the Bonapartes departed like a flock of noisy crows that has stripped a tree barren of fruit.

Twenty-two

Paris, 1797~1798

As winter approached, Napoleon and Josephine returned to Paris, where he was needed to resume his duties for the Directory. The newly arrived couple found themselves glorified. The nine years of the French Revolution had been wiped clean by Napoleon, whose latest acquisitions for France — Belgium and the west bank of the Rhine — had transformed him into a legend.

The Directory, the Revolution's tottering government, was weakening each day. Paul Barras, always a strong republican, was still in charge. However, political factions were trying to create yet another government. The last thing France needed was another revolution, so when the streets of Paris rang with cries of "Long live Bonaparte," it was clear to many that a savior had come. Hearing Bonaparte's praises shouted at every corner, Barras had reason to wonder — the little general he'd groomed for greatness was beginning to eclipse his mentor.

For Josephine, the remembered nights of the villa, the tranquil garden, and the swans in the pond faded into a dim memory. Paris claimed her attention as never before. Everything was changed, and changing. Even the rue de Chantereine had been renamed rue de la Victoire, in honor of Napoleon. Uniformed guards were now stationed to keep the curious from scaling their hedge. Still, people were always straining their eyes to catch a glimpse of the illustrious general and his beautiful wife.

Bonaparte accepted his celebrity better than Josephine. He seemed, in fact, to require it. Nor did the common luxuries of the past please him anymore. As the great conqueror of Italy and the peacekeeper of Austria, Bonaparte demanded more and more honor and money — and he got it. The ailing Directory saw him as their hope and savior; therefore, they refused him nothing.

So now Josephine's modest house was remodeled according to Napoleon's specifications. Large, open reception rooms replaced Josephine's quiet little artistic salon. As soon as the modifications were done, the house was filled with important visitors, public officials, and foreign delegations. It resembled an embassy more than a home.

At first horrified by the way her private life was made public, Josephine did what she'd done her whole life — shed her fear and molded herself to suit the times. Floating from party to party in an exotic West Indian turban, Josephine seemed to be one of the members of the new aristocracy. This was something she'd always aspired to, and it made her feel good to be so admired.

One night Napoleon and Josephine sat together by candlelight. His lips softened into a smile. Then he touched his nose to hers, and he kissed her once, twice, three times. She kissed him back after the third time. He returned that kiss with a fourth. "Shall we go to bed?" he asked. She nodded.

Once under the covers, Napoleon sighed.

"Now what is wrong?" Josephine asked.

"Oh," he sighed again. "I love you more than you shall ever love me."

"No, you don't," she said, her heavily lashed eyes twinkling. "You love but one thing, Bonaparte."

"And that is?"

"Your lucky star — your destiny. That you love more than me — even more than *you*. More than anything. It will be your ruin."

Napoleon turned his head around and sat up. "That candle gleams right in my eye," he whined.

"Then blow it out, silly!"

Instead, Napoleon groaned and settled back onto his pillow.

"What is it now?" she asked.

He looked grimly at his wife. "Some light is always good," he said.

"You *are* haunted," she told him. "Otherwise you'd snuff out that candle and go straight to sleep."

All at once, Bonaparte jumped out of bed, hopped over to the desk, and pinched out the candle flame. The bedroom darkened.

Napoleon got back into bed. When he'd settled down again, he asked Josephine, "Do you want to come?"

"To Egypt?"

"Yes."

"To watch men die — sometimes ours, sometimes theirs?"

"Yes. That's the magnificence of it."

Josephine said into the dark, "I shall never, *ever* understand you, Bonaparte."

"Nor I you."

"I know," Josephine sighed. "So why do we even try?"

Napoleon said gently, "It does not matter if we

understand each other. What matters is that we stay in love. You see, Josephine, the truth is that when you are at my side and not someone else's, nothing bad can happen to me."

"Then you must not go to Egypt," Josephine advised.

Napoleon lay back on his pillow. "I must," he said.

"Then I should go with you."

"No, it's too dangerous," Napoleon replied, reconsidering.

"What about Eugène?"

"I will watch over him every moment. Don't worry, he will be safe in my care." Then he leaned close and kissed her. "And I will be safe in your care, if you think of me often enough."

Twenty-three

Alexandria, Egypt, 1798

Although Josephine objected, it was Talleyrand, France's foreign minister, who applauded Napoleon for his expedition against Egypt. *The Directory, Talleyrand thought, will be well rid of the heroic general. Things are confusing enough without Napoleon being ushered into the government by popular demand. People are already saying, "Make the general a director!"*

With Napoleon gone, I will maneuver things my way.

"Why don't you attack the British?" he asked the general one day.

Napoleon answered, "How I would love to, but they're almost indomitable on the sea, which is why I want to go to Malta, and from there to Egypt. If I can conquer Malta and Alexandria, Britain will be my next conquest."

Talleyrand saw the gleam in Napoleon's eye, and he had no doubt of his implacable will. What the little man wanted he got. England. Not since Alexander had an army landed on Britain's shores. "I would enjoy seeing England pay at last for stealing our American colonies," Talleyrand said with a grin. "But you are right, there is much to do. Striking at England through Malta and Egypt is not a bad idea."

Napoleon said, "From Egypt I can go straight to India, where England sits as proudly as an old lioness. Without India, England is lost."

Without Napoleon here to haunt me, I shall make certain the Directory stays in one piece, Talleyrand thought, all the while smiling courteously at his ambitious general. *But what if he should succeed? When he returns, he'll be no less than a king.* This gave Talleyrand pause for thought.

*   *   *

Surveying the African coast for the first time, Napoleon trembled with excitement. Indeed, this was Africa. He'd dreamed of this moment since he was a boy at military school, reading about his hero, Alexander of Macedonia. Now, as he was about to set foot in Alexandria, perhaps to walk in the very footsteps of that great conqueror, a momentary sense of humility overcame him. But it lasted only a moment.

"What riches await me?" he wondered aloud. "What priceless perfumes, linens, jewels, metals, ores, artifacts, and spices? What art treasures? What manuscripts of antiquity?" He paced the deck of his ship while his eye roved the dry landscape of dull gold sand. "There lies the ancient city where the Greek savants founded mathematics, astronomy, philosophy, and the universities whose books still bear the names of Ptolemy, Aristotle, Diogenes, Socrates."

Napoleon took a deep breath, inhaling the moist humus of the African coast.

"I have but one thought," he told his secretary. "To crush the Ottoman Empire and to drive out the ruling Turks, those so-called Mamelukes. Beyond that we shall eliminate the British, who think this territory should, by right, belong to them. They imagine themselves rulers of the Mediterranean. I shall teach them a lesson. Once again France will have an empire in the East."

"And then what, sir?"

"First conquer, then civilize," Napoleon said smartly as the ship's sails flapped in the Alexandrian breeze.

"How soon do you expect to conquer them, sir?" the secretary questioned as he leaned on the railing of *L'Orient*.

"Yes," echoed Eugène, who pressed himself against Bonaparte's other side. "How soon, sir?"

With hands behind his back, Bonaparte grinned, his large eyes glinting with an insatiable appetite. "Tonight," he answered.

And so it was: just after midnight. Bonaparte was on

shore under a shallow yellow moon. More than four thousand foot soldiers were with him. The conquering had begun.

By midday, as the sun bore down, Alexandria fell to the French.

By day's end, Bonaparte inquired of Eugène, whose face was streaked with sweat and dirt but no blood, "How many French officers have died?"

"Six," Eugène replied.

"Infantry?"

"Fifteen dead."

"Wounded?"

"Twenty."

Bonaparte smiled like a cat. "How many Turks dead?"

Eugène muttered, "I don't know, sir."

"How many are left in the city?"

Eugène's brow furrowed. Shaking his head, he said, "I don't know that, either, sir." But then his face got tight and he asked, "Do you think I have done well, sir?"

Bonaparte gazed at Eugène as if for the first time.

For a moment, he did nothing. The two stood motionless. Then Napoleon wrapped his arms around the boy and kissed him on both cheeks several times. In between kisses, while still clasping Eugène's head in his hands, Napoleon inquired, "Have you killed anyone?"

"Did I?" Eugène's face clouded with shame. "I — don't think so," he mumbled. Eugène looked at his dust-covered boots. One of them had a sword's gash in it — a gash he'd accidentally delivered himself.

"Don't worry, you will!" Bonaparte promised, his broad forehead shining, his face glowing.

To the question of enemy dead, Bonaparte's secretary found the truth. "Most of them fled into the night when we scaled the walls," he told Bonaparte.

Napoleon jammed his right hand into the front of his half-buttoned waistcoat. He rubbed his stomach, and belched. "We've eaten nothing," he said. His stomach growled. The fires of the city lapped at the stars. The whole thing had been a little too easy, he thought, a little too smooth. He required more grit, more blood, as payment for his "star." "My star dines on bones, not beauty," he said with an angry sigh.

One week later Bonaparte and his forces marched into Cairo, which fell as swiftly as Alexandria had. Again, it was a little too easy for Napoleon's liking, but it did seem as if nothing could stop him, and that his star was shining firmly in his favor. But then fate conspired to do exactly the opposite. The French forces had little or no food, and Bonaparte wrote, *We drink nothing but brackish water, often not even that; we have to eat dogs, donkeys, and camels.* Yet while he was busy on the land, Admiral Nelson, the brilliant English sea captain, attacked the French fleet at Aboukir Bay and completely destroyed it. Secretly, these new hardships were just what Napoleon had been asking for.

"Obstacles," he told Eugène, "make men large or small, and without them man is not there at all."

However, there came the greatest and most insurmountable of all difficulties.

Disease — the plague — struck down soldier after soldier.

In a matter of days thousands of French solders died. Barefoot and already broken by the 110-degree days, the troops crumbled. They died from malnutrition as well as heatstroke and illness. Bonaparte stormed into the hospital one day and hauled a corpse outside so all could see he was not afraid of the plague. He believed more soldiers were dying of fear than from the disease itself. And as always when Bonaparte did something rash, his men rallied. "Even death backs away from Bonaparte," a soldier said. Others repeated the statement until more men got out of their sickbeds and swore their allegiance to the republic of France.

Thus Napoleon marched on.

To the directors in Paris, Napoleon sent his own praises of himself:

It is likely enough that when you read this letter I shall be standing on the ruins of the city of Solomon.

And he added, *I am as terrible as the fire from heaven.*

But the directors didn't believe it. They'd heard about the destruction of the French fleet at Aboukir from English newspapers and received letters telling of the plague and of the Egyptian resistance in small desert towns that Bonaparte couldn't bomb into submission. Rumors went all about France. Cannons, it was said, cracked from overuse and had to be abandoned. Worst of all, the directors learned, the sum total of Bonaparte's tribute, his gift to France was boxes of books written in ancient Greek.

It was also rumored — and much to his detriment — that Bonaparte had lovers and was growing remiss in his duties as general. Scandal sheets played upon the fact that he'd taken up with the wife of Lieutenant Foures, a woman he'd nicknamed Cleopatra. She was a beautiful young lady — ten years younger than Bonaparte — with blond hair that fell to her waist.

Thus did the Parisian rumor mill grind out story after

story. The sad truth was that most of these tales were somewhat, if not all, true. The only thing completely made up was Bonaparte's lax behavior as a general. He didn't have a soft bone in his body, as anyone who knew him was well aware.

Twenty-four

Paris, 1799

All during his Egyptian campaign, Josephine had been having bad dreams about Napoleon. She saw him in the desert with a gaping hole in his chest. Beside her fallen husband was a golden lion slouching indolently while overhead black birds of doom wheeled across the empty sphere of the sky. All around Bonaparte were sand dunes, desolate and dead, in the Egyptian sun. Josephine woke from this nightmare, crying out but with no sound coming from her mouth.

One day after suffering the same dream over and over the night before, Josephine set off with Mimi to consult Madame Lenormand, who was well known in Paris as the Sorceress.

"There are many ways we can reach your husband,"

Madame Lenormand said in a husky voice when Josephine visited her, as she had many times before. The young gypsy-eyed woman wore a hooded cape, the inside of which was scarlet, the exterior black velvet with gold piping. The Sorceress's white wig was sinuously tied with coils of indigo snakeskin. She was charming in a macabre way, and her apartment reflected her personality, as it was designed to look like the interior of a silk-lined coffin. The walls were puffed and buttoned silk made to look exactly like the final resting place of a corpse.

"I have the same frightening dream night after night," Josephine confessed to Madame Lenormand. "I see my husband in the desert of the East, and he is wholly without a heart."

Madame Lenormand raised her ankle-length skirt and adjusted her position on the sofa. Josephine and Mimi glanced unavoidably at the Sorceress's shoes. They were leather-laced sandals that twined, snakelike, to her calves. But the most amazing thing was her toes, each of which was encircled with an emerald toe ring.

Madame Lenormand smiled. Her wide-set, tranquil eyes were brown, green, or gray, depending on the light in the room. Now, because the chamber was darkly lighted, Madame Lenormand's eyes were the color of ashes. In the tapered light, she moved her thin, well-ringed fingers, fluttering them like night moths.

"Let us see what is to be by looking into your palm." Then the Sorceress clasped Josephine's hand and held it open.

"Why, you're as cold as ice," Madame Lenormand said in surprise. "Are you so afraid of the truth?"

Josephine felt her heart jump. "Quite the contrary. I'm committed to the truth." She glanced at Mimi, who replied with a nod.

"Then," said the Sorceress, "let the truth come forth."

"And cleanse my dreams," Josephine put in.

Madame Lenormand closed her eyes. A moment later, her head bowed, but her fingers were still attached to Josephine's. In a slow, sleepy voice she spoke of Napoleon as if she were there with him in Egypt.

"I see him now, as he is. While the others are asleep, he is wakeful. There are tents as far as the eye can see. They are like flowers that bloom in the moon. His alone has light in it. He goes forth, stands outside his tent, stares at the stars. His eyes are fixed upon a certain star that is twinkling above him in the firmament. Now he returns through the door of his tent. Takng up a ruler he draws lines upon a map. He glances at his watch. Now he goes outside to regard the horizon, then the heavens. He returns to his table. Sitting down in a chair, he examines his watch. Then he is on his feet once more and off to the tent door and back again to the chair. He puts his face into his folded arms and rests his head on the table. His strong profile is lighted by the single lamp. His dark head is buried now."

Josephine, who listened, amazed, without stirring, opened her mouth and spoke with the tenderest concern. "Is he all right? Is he wounded? Where is he? I must know."

Madame Lenormand bobbed her head at the intrusion of Josephine's voice, and went on with her monologue. "I see him carving something in the arm of his chair." She shook her head then, and added, "No, he's not carving, he's slashing. In all ways, the man resembles a small boy."

Josephine could not help herself — she laughed.

"The time of night is late," said Madame Lenormand. "All the generals are soundly sleeping. Ah, I see him writing a letter. From time to time, he cleans his quill on his knee britches. His right leg — it's smeared with ink spots."

Josephine laughed again. The Sorceress ignored her.

"It is the time just before daybreak. His pen is nibbling at the paper like a hungry mouse. Oh, *sacre bleu*, the general is fading, fading, gone." Her voice, burned to a soft breath of ash, ceased.

Josephine looked at Mimi, whose face, resting on her open hand, registered no expression beyond attentiveness. Madame Lenormand drew a long breath. Then exhaling through her nostrils, she resumed her slow, syrupy recitation.

"I see a woman now . . . with hair long and luxuriant. Her face is young and beautiful. A letter is in her hand. The top of it is addressed to — I cannot quite see what it is, or to whom —"

Then the confident voice returned.

"*Cleopatra, my Cleopatra,* that is what it says. The young woman is smiling and the letter is signed *Caesar*. At her bare feet I see a live spotted cat of the desert. Behind her back is a marble pool from Roman times."

The Sorceress covered her face in her hands. She seemed to be losing the vision, and was trying to hold on to it in some way. The tick of her mantel clock repeated its endless refrain. Then Madame Lenormand opened her eyes.

"Have I said anything useful?" she asked, blinking her long dark lashes.

* * *

Josephine did not usually have a jealous nature, and she was able to accept Madame Lenormand's vision as truth. Napoleon's lover was with him in Egypt. But where?

Turkey, Russia, Sardinia, Naples, Sweden, Austria, Germany, England, Prussia, and Russia all wondered the same thing. Looking for any pretext to declare war on France, they awaited the little general.

Where was Bonaparte? Alive or dead? No one knew for sure.

Even Josephine didn't understand why he hadn't written her in so many months. *Am I so far from his thoughts?* she wondered. *Is he so far from mine? No, I am as faithful as Bonaparte wants me to be . . . so why has he not written to me?*

Then one day Josephine went to the home of Paul Barras to try to quell the rumors about Bonaparte's death. While waiting in his salon she overheard him say to another director, "If the general is not dead in Egypt, he is certainly dead to France."

This sent her home in tears. Still, she told Mimi, "If he were dead, I would know it. He is alive."

Although she occasionally felt the sting of jealousy, Josephine did not struggle with love and loyalty. She loved Bonaparte in his absence, and as his enemies amassed, more than ever before.

"I really love him," she told Mimi.

"Of course you do."

"No, I mean, I really and truly love him. I don't know why, but I do, I do."

Twenty-five

Paris & Egypt, 1799

Josephine's life without Napoleon was harder for her than for him. Suddenly she found herself with more debts than diamonds. She told Mimi, "I know what I am going to do. I'm going to buy another house."

"Your love of country estates is your undoing, Josephine."

Before he had left for Egypt, Josephine had tried to interest Napoleon in a beautiful old estate called Malmaison. Bonaparte had refused.

"Be content with what you have," he'd said curtly.

But while he was gone, Josephine longed to get out of the city. She wanted to get away from gossip and intrigue. Every day the notices of her husband's death in Egypt appeared in the broadsheets. So the grand old château of Malmaison, a decaying three-story house on three hundred acres overlooking the Seine, became her obsession. *If I can get into Malmaison, everything will be all right,* she told herself.

As it happened, Malmaison belonged to Josephine long before her husband was rumored to be sailing home to France. She borrowed beyond her ability to pay anyone back, bought the old, crumbling house on the Seine, and settled peacefully into it. Now she had something to really fear from her husband: the purchase of a debt-ridden house that he'd forbidden her to buy.

For ten months Bonaparte had no news from Paris. Then one morning in Cairo he saw a copy of the *Journal de Frankfort* and realized how bad the home news was. Overcome with despondency, Napoleon asked his secretary if he'd seen the paper. "I handed it to you, sir, I didn't read it. Is there bad news?"

Bonaparte said in despair, "All Italy is lost. A

Russian and Austrian army has driven us out. All my victories — vanished. The Directory — overturned — and new directors put in place."

The secretary was astonished.

Napoleon continued, "Barras remains, but he's the only one left whom I know and trust. Right now, to tell you the truth, I don't know whose side he's on . . . mine, I hope. Meanwhile, Russia and Austria are advancing on France. Our world is collapsing, and we're not even there to protect it!"

In truth, Napoleon was seeing for the first time what Europeans had known for a whole year. They knew all about Admiral Nelson crushing the French at Aboukir. There was now an alliance between Britain, Austria, Turkey, Russia, and the kingdom of Naples, and it aimed to exact a huge reprisal on France, or rather, Napoleon.

"We must leave Egypt at once," Napoleon said, pounding his open hand with his fist.

"What of our troops and the military campaign?" his secretary asked.

"Forget them! We have to get home — now!"

Leaving behind infantry, officers, and supplies and barely enough munitions to stave off a counterattack should one arise, Bonaparte abandoned his Egyptian dream and hurried home to Europe. He took with him Eugène and a small staff. Egypt was left in the capable hands of a French general whose orders were given in a curt note that more or less read, "Hold the fort . . . we'll be back."

A favorable wind and a merciful fog sent Napoleon's frigate, the *Muiron*, out of the Nile delta and off to the southeast, where they dodged the British warships that were patrolling like sharks all over the Mediterranean in search of Napoleon.

After four weeks of rough weather, Bonaparte arrived in the harbor of Ajaccio on the pine-scented shore of Corsica, his birthplace. Hundreds of small fishing boats clustered around the French vessels. The Corsicans wanted to see their famous countryman, but Bonaparte found it difficult to be sociable. The last thing he wanted to indulge in right now was undeserved adulation.

"They love you, sir," his secretary said. "You can't fault them for that."

Some days later Bonaparte arrived at the French harbor of Frejas. "Send a courier to the new Directory right away," he commanded his secretary. "Tell them I'm going to be in Paris before they know it."

He was off by coach before the frigate was unloaded, traveling north and west toward Nevers, a route not usually taken to Paris. However, though he wanted secrecy, he got the opposite — huge outpourings of love from every villager along the way. Sometimes they surrounded his carriage singing out, "Long live Bonaparte! Long live our father!"

The moment she heard that her husband was in France, Josephine called for her carriage, and she and Hortense went directly to Lyons to meet Bonaparte on the road. Hoping to intercept him along the way, she ordered her coachman to travel at top speed.

That day, though, the couple's star of destiny was not looking out for either of them. Galloping on the Burgundy road, Josephine completely missed her husband. He, racing on the Nevers road, bypassed her and reached rue de la Victoire in Paris ahead of schedule.

Not seeing Josephine but reading a gossip column in the paper about a strange affair she apparently was having with one of his aides threw him into a fit of rage. What he'd always suspected — that his wife was unfaithful — was true, or so he thought. This was complicated, in his own mind, by his own unfaithfulness in Egypt, something for which he now felt a rising and inadmissible guilt.

Worst of all, Bonaparte was treated to an empty house. Famished and exhausted, he threw open the door of every room while calling out, "Josephine, Josephine!"

At last he came into the kitchen, where Mimi told him that Josephine was on her way to Lyons in the hope of greeting him before anyone else did. Napoleon sank onto a sofa, boots on, muttering to himself about perfidious wives. Then snorting like a wounded bull, he stomped off to the bedroom, leaving Eugène to muddle over what to do now that they were home.

After locking the bedroom door, Bonaparte went straight to bed, but he didn't sleep. Eugène and Mimi heard him talking to himself, swearing oaths and fuming over his wife's infidelity. Napoleon's brother Joseph showed up forthwith. He was usually the one who smoothed Bonaparte's nerves, but this time when he knocked on the bedroom door and announced himself, Napoleon shouted, "Be gone!"

As the night wore on, Napoleon's sisters came by, pressed their heads to the door, and made accusations against their despised sister-in-law. Their whining and wheedling made Bonaparte angrier, and he screamed at them to leave the house, which they did, reluctantly.

Napoleon showed his face only once — to ask a housemaid to prepare his bath. Once he lay soaking, his temper started to subside. He submerged himself until the hot water was cold and his skin was whiter than a pickled octopus.

"I'll divorce her — that's what I'll do!" Napoleon vowed as he got out of the bath and into his tricolor robe.

His secretary came by and pleaded for Napoleon to open the door. He had news he thought Napoleon wanted to hear. "Your wife has just come into the courtyard, sir."

Hearing this, Bonaparte threw off his robe and stood naked in the candlelight. He regarded himself in a gilded mirror on the wall. Suddenly the sight of his naked body made him burst out laughing. He howled and clapped and danced.

"What is it, sir?" the secretary asked.

Napoleon said, "I think I just saw the devil."

Twenty-six

Paris, 1799

"Let me in, Bonaparte, I can explain everything," Josephine cried.

"I will never forgive you," he fired back.

"For what?" she entreated.

Bonaparte, still naked on the other side of the locked door, went back to the mirror.

You're much too thin, he said to himself. *Eyes sunken, hair gone — better comb it straight down to hide the baldness.*

He pressed his palm against his locks to flatten them down over his wide brow.

My mouth is still symmetrical. Napoleon continued his self-evaluation. He grinned like a horse and inspected his teeth.

"What are you mumbling? I can't hear you," Josephine cried.

"Go away," Napoleon bellowed.

At the same time he threw his olive green riding coat over his narrow shoulders and began the furious brushing of his teeth.

"You're as tall as a worm," he muttered. "No, you're better than that — you're a mouse." He grumbled at his unsightly reflection, "A prissy little mouse with no mustache." This made him laugh, and thus he examined his teeth again. "Ah, but you do have a scimitar," he went on, his mouth still foaming with tooth powder. Then he strode into the bedroom and strapped on his military belt with the monogrammed buckle. Behind the belt he slipped the scimitar scabbard. Then, back to the mirror for another look.

"Whatever are you doing, Bonaparte?" called Josephine.

"You need trousers," he told the mirror. On the seat of a brocaded chair, his dirty clothes lay in a heap. He glanced at them, then flipped the chair with his bare foot. Throwing open a drawer, he grabbed a clean pair of knee britches. Tugging them on, he tossed off the riding coat, went back to the mirror, and thrust out his chest.

"Oh, you great white mouse with a scimitar," Napoleon said and laughed. "All you need is a turban!"

"*Please*, Bonaparte, let me in!" Josephine begged.

Adding to her strident cry was Hortense's. Eugène's, too. And Mimi's. All of them begged for his release as Josephine's parrot, having been awakened, screamed bloody murder.

Bonaparte's flinty voice told them all to go away.

In the end, they sat on the floor and waited in silence.

Hours later, the door opened. Bonaparte stepped out all dressed in red velvet, as if on his way to a coronation. He greeted everyone calmly and cordially.

The terrible storm in his head seemed to have gone away. A little later, when the others had gone to bed, Bonaparte crawled into Josephine's lap as he had always done in the past. She stroked his forehead and felt him melt like a child.

"For a while," he murmured, "I was free from the obstacles of this pitiful, irksome civilization. Oh, I was filled with dreams. . . ."

"In Egypt?"

"Yes, in Egypt." His eyes widened. "I saw myself founding a new religion, my men marching into Asia while I rode upon an elephant." He sat up suddenly, very animated. "I have a turban — do you want me to put it on?"

"I could wear mine, too," she said smiling.

"I could read you passages from the Koran — it's beautiful poetry, you know."

"I know, I know," she repeated, stroking his head.

He got calm again and lay down in her lap.

Josephine read him stanzas from the heroic poetry of Ossian, all about war and death and ghosts. Bonaparte listened and his eyes danced with phantoms of the past, specters that lived for him only in language.

"Who," Josephine asked, "is that strange man sleeping in front of our bedroom door? I almost tripped over him."

"That," answered Bonaparte, "is Roustam, my bodyguard."

"He certainly doesn't look like any of us."

"That's because he's a Mameluke, the people I conquered in Egypt. You can't conquer him, though. He's more loyal to me than . . ."

"I am?" Josephine queried mockingly.

Bonaparte, buttoning his shirt and sipping his morning tea, made no response.

That night, however, Bonaparte slept with two pistols under his pillow. "My overthrow of this worthless Directory is coming," he said to Josephine. "But don't let it worry you."

The next morning Talleyrand, the secretive, wise, and sullen foreign minister, was waiting for him in the salon. Talleyrand spoke, his voice cold and reproving.

"The soul of France is in danger. All that you've done is about to be *undone*. We must go to the Tuileries at once. There is no one there who can govern any longer. At someone's whim we could all be out of office."

"Or *in*," Napoleon said with a sneer. "I'll meet my opposition head on." His eyes glittered. He knew this was his chance to rise from general to the more powerful, political role of director. He might never separate himself from the army, but here was his first opportunity to seize the reins of the government, and to take control of the whole country.

"Very well," Talleyrand said, straightening his coat. "I see your intent. It's good, the people need to believe in someone, and you're the only bright star in a dark sky." Talleyrand had accepted the inevitable. Napoleon's presence was still the most powerful political force in France.

Bonaparte, sitting on the sofa, crossed his legs and ate an apple. For the rest of that day, he listened to Talleyrand's encouragement and advice. After the minister dismissed himself, his silk coattails whisking, a bevy of politicians passed in and out of the gate of rue de la Victoire. Bonaparte met them, too, heard their woes, each in kind, and went on to his next task without a pause.

Like marionettes, the brothers Bonaparte, Joseph and Lucien, also put in their appearance. Their solution for what ailed the republic was for Napoleon to divorce Josephine.

Napoleon remained as listless as if his brothers were speaking of the weather. He told them he'd think about it, and moved on to other things. The things that he moved on to were swift and dangerous, and his entire career rested on their outcome. Realizing that he had enemies who were trying to oust him, Napoleon declared that "foreign influences"— spies from England — were trying to kick him out of France.

Napoleon was believed. He could count on his growing popularity with the people, if not with the governing bodies that held sway over politics. The people loved him. They also feared, more than anything, foreign powers and the influence they bore. The French feared the English, in particular. They were aggressors who were seeking any excuse to send their armies to the continent.

All Napoleon had to do at a government meeting was say that his life was being threatened by "English agents" and suddenly, everyone was on his side. Those who weren't for him watched and waited to see what he would do next. What he did was establish himself overnight as first consul. In a brave and risky move, Napoleon appointed himself the most powerful man in all of France. Now the government answered only to him. He had done this in less than twenty-four hours, and even his wife, Josephine, didn't know how he'd pulled it off so smoothly.

Twenty - seven

Luxembourg & The Tuileries, 1799~1800

On 10 November 1799, Napoleon overthrew the Directory and appointed himself first consul. He was now but one step away from declaring himself emperor and his plans to reconquer Italy had begun. Meanwhile, he and Josephine moved into the old royal palace of Luxembourg. There Napoleon reshaped the government by getting rid of the former directors and appointing two consuls directly under his command. In addition, he awarded himself the power of appointing all officials from small-town mayors to high ministers. Napoleon set up a legislature that consisted of a tribunate that debated the laws. But, although there was a congress and a senate, nothing got through without his approval, so in effect, this made Bonaparte's new government a dictatorship. No one complained, though, unless it was the deposed Barras and a few other disgruntled ministers who both hated and feared him.

The main thing was that order had been restored and Napoleon was the apotheosis of that harmony. The people were appeased. That was what mattered most. "More revolts are caused by lack of bread than by political causes," Napoleon said. "If my people are fed, they won't care what's being done at the Tuileries." Sometimes at night Bonaparte roamed the streets of Paris in disguise, seeking out the opinions of the common man, sometimes asking, "What do you think of that joker Bonaparte?" The answers, which usually cast him as the savior of France, made Napoleon laugh all the way home.

When he wasn't dictating letters, he was nibbling at his nails and whittling on the arms of his favorite chair with a penknife. Josephine often found him singing some rooms away from her while his just-vacated chair remained in his office with a penknife jutting out of one of its arms.

They had spent only a few months at Luxembourg before moving into the refurbished Tuileries. Then Napoleon with characteristic suddenness was off to the Swiss Alps, and his second Italian campaign was under way. Two months later, he returned home victorious. Once again, Italy was under his thumb.

All of Paris turned out to see Napoleon — wherever he went, whatever he did.

Standing on his office balcony at the Tuileries overlooking a courtyard crowd, Napoleon said to Talleyrand, "I have no use for this."

"You've no use for what?"

Bonaparte waved to his admirers, his half smile barely concealing his boredom. "The battle's done. What else is there but the battle?"

Talleyrand uttered a little "Oh."

Bonaparte looked at him with annoyance. "You don't believe me?"

"I think you love all of it — if it's going your way. And I think you hate it when it doesn't."

Napoleon answered, "I enjoy the martial music that accompanies these affairs."

He turned his back on the crowd. "Don't we have some work to do?"

Talleyrand said, "This *is* your work."

"No, Talleyrand, this is *your* work. Mine is with my daughters."

"Your daughters?"

Napoleon smiled as if he were letting Talleyrand in on a secret, which, in fact, he was. "My daughters I call them because we are so close. But really, they are just my cannons."

"And you call them your daughters."

"Exactly."

Talleyrand shrugged. There was no accounting for

Napoleon Bonaparte. And it was a good thing that, for the most part, all of France gloried in their ruler, a man as unfathomable as the weather — and yet everybody thought they knew him so well.

That night, wearing a red madras scarf Créole-style over her head, Josephine read to Bonaparte from Livy. Her silvery voice, soft and low, told of the exploits of Hannibal. When she read to him, Napoleon was in heaven. There was a certain lilt, a singing rise and fall to the way she gave voice to words, that thrilled him.

"I could listen to you read forever," he murmured, his head on her lap. He lay there in his purple velvet robe admiring her curves, her face.

"Do you like the way I redesigned your bedroom?" she asked. "Do you like the striped camp tent that goes over your bed?"

"Josephine, *mon coeur*, you think of everything," he said.

She read on, and he lay there under the spell of her West Indian rhythm. However, behind his closed eyes,

Napoleon saw frozen rivers and endless mountains buried in snow, and he saw the heavy tread of Hannibal's elephants tramping through a white wilderness that now belonged to France.

That Christmas Eve Bonaparte's carriage was on its way to the Paris opera. He did not want to go at first, but Josephine argued that he had to put in an appearance.

"At my last *appearance* I was nearly murdered," he said.

"They caught the assassins and we have security tonight," she insisted.

Napoleon paced the hall of their apartment at the Tuileries.

And though Josephine wore a beautiful Constantinople shawl, which Napoleon had brought back to her from Egypt, and which she'd worn just to please him, he had nothing good to say about it.

"Your dress is not open enough in front," he argued.

"It's cold," Hortense said, taking her mother's side.

"Yes, it's *always* something," he grumbled.

"Please, Bonaparte," Josephine begged, "it's Haydn's *Creation*. Can we please not be late?"

She rubbed his cheek with her hand. "Don't worry. Everything will be all right."

Looking disgruntled and worried, he finally shrugged and, without further comment, pulled his battered tricorn over his head and marched outside in a heavy, dark overcoat. The air was cold and crisp with a hint of snowflakes.

"See," Josephine said as they got into their carriages, "you can even see the stars."

The rhythmic clop of hooves and the easy creak of leather put Bonaparte into a better frame of mind. He imagined himself on campaign. Soon he was dozing, dreaming of Hannibal's elephants.

Behind Napoleon's carriage, a second coach carried Josephine, Hortense, and General Murat's wife, Caroline, who was also Napoleon's sister.

As the carriages headed toward the rue de la Loi, there was suddenly a white flash, followed by an explosion that slammed into the carriages of the Bonaparte family. A horse and cart were ripped apart by the blast — head and hooves flying off in different directions. Two or three buildings blew up, bursting into flame. People screamed. Bonaparte stumbled out of his carriage, dazed but unhurt. On the cobbled street, twelve people lay dead. Twenty-eight others were wounded. Some crawled about in the debris, moaning.

In Josephine's carriage, no one except Hortense was injured. She held up her bleeding hand, which had been grazed by a flying shard of glass. Caroline, eight months pregnant, groaned and complained that her stomach hurt. Dizzily she walked in circles as Josephine tried to keep her on her feet.

The heavy, mustached minister of police, Joseph Fouché, showed up and boasted confidently to Napoleon that the criminals would soon be caught. "I can assure you," he said, "that it shall be so." Bonaparte looked skeptically at him. "And how do you propose to catch these invisible assassins?" he demanded.

The police minister, standing in blood, said, "I'm going to put the murderer's mare back together, one piece at a time if I have to."

Napoleon, his ears still ringing, asked what good that would do.

Fouché replied, "*Someone* will remember whose horse it was."

"What a mess," Bonaparte remarked. "I was dreaming of a battlefield, and now I'm standing in one."

"Leave it to me," the policeman advised. "I know what I'm doing."

Bonaparte adjusted his hat. "Are you well enough to proceed, Josephine? This is your night."

"I hear nothing but bells ringing," she replied, holding her head in her hands.

"That will coincide well with Haydn, I think," Napoleon added with a wink, and a moment later he was in his coach heading for the opera house. He got there ahead of the others and seemed to all who saw him very chipper about things. No one suspected what had just happened.

Josephine, a freshly bandaged Hortense, and Caroline got to their seats with difficulty, but they, too, arrived and were doing their best to overcome their discomfort.

As they were shown to their seats, Napoleon remarked to Josephine, "Well, it *is* worth it, isn't it?"

"I don't know yet, I haven't heard the music."

"I was talking about all the applause we're getting, *mon amour*."

"Oh, but they love you, Bonaparte," Josephine said wearily.

"They have gunpowder in their pockets," he replied. "Not all, but some."

"Just a few . . . but those are the ones you have to worry about."

* * *

In the quiet of their bedroom late that night, Bonaparte admitted that this murderous plot, like the one before it, *was a token of the English, not French disdain*. His worst enemies, he believed, were in England.

"I hate the English," he muttered to Josephine. "Don't you?"

"I don't *know* them."

While she slept, he spent the whole of the night at his desk, drawing a massive warship that would transport a half-million soldiers and arms to the shores of England. His pen scratched in every detail. At last he stood back and admired his artistry. "This beauty will be the end of the English," he swore to the candle. "That is, if we can ever lift her off the paper and set her in the sea."

He snuffed out the candle as the sun came up.

Twenty-eight

Paris, 1803~1804

To the people of France, Napoleon and Josephine were the perfect couple. But as their national popularity increased each month, their marriage, always under the public eye, started to fall apart. Napoleon — after two major assassination attempts by the English — was suspicious of everyone and everything. Wary and unpredictable, he prowled about Malmaison with one hand on his spyglass and the other on his snuffbox. Between peeping and sniffing, he paced from one room to another, his footfalls echoing, creaking, shuffling, or shambling, and his tuneless, discordant whistling telling Josephine of his wildly manic moods. Although he loved the way Josephine had decorated Malmaison, he loathed the way she'd purchased it behind his back and how she'd put her household further into debt with another mortgage. Still, he let it go in his characteristic fashion — after blowing up and making her cry. When they'd kissed and made up, he paid for her extravagances and forgot all about it.

Summer or winter, Napoleon seemed cold-blooded. Often his lips were blue and his face white, or as some observed, slightly yellowish. Building a bonfire in mid-August, he liked to stand in a statuesque pose watching the leaping flames, as if fire, and nothing else, were his true ally. In front of the massive fireplace, dictating letter after letter, Napoleon held forth in his usual tireless way until a young servant brought him a cup of hot tea.

Anything that he'd ordered but not supervised caused him to cock an eyebrow in alarm. One day, he had a fit over a teacup.

"Where did this come from?" he demanded.

"From the pantry," said the frightened servant girl.

In a fit of rage, Napoleon seized the suspect cup and saucer and hurled them against the wall.

During this trying time, Josephine had her own

troubles — from acute headaches that sent her to bed, to her husband's wild and weird affairs and deceptions. But she spent hours among her flowers. In the embrace of fragrant tropical scents she forgot herself. Napoleon, for all of his devilment, loved the pleasant atmosphere of Malmaison. He liked to go hunting and picnicking, and he often played with Josephine's gazelles.

One night Napoleon asked his secretary to show him Josephine's "secret debts," the ones that had cost him so dearly. Josephine's botanical gardens and nature park were being expanded, so that, by now, there was no place like them in all of Europe.

"She has all manner of charges, sir."

"Name them."

"Well, her fineries include hundreds of hats with herons' plumes —"

"Dead herons?"

"The live kind do not sit on hats, sir," the secretary said.

"No, they live in my wife's pond." Napoleon clamped his lips tight. "What are these things worth?" he asked.

"The plumes?"

Bonaparte nodded.

The secretary touched his manicured finger to his little ledger book.

"Ten thousand francs."

Napoleon strode across the salon in low, slipperlike shoes of Spanish leather. He wore a red velvet jacket with gold embroidery and buttons. No more the sloppy dresser, Bonaparte wore his clothes like the emperor that he imagined himself to be.

"Altogether how much did Josephine owe before we cleared her accounts without her knowledge?"

The tired secretary removed his spectacles and rubbed his eyes. "Well, we settled, sir, at six hundred thousand. Yet you will recall she owed well over a million." The man expected Bonaparte to lash out — or, at the very least, to take a random pistol shot out the window.

But Bonaparte was not one to be counted on for anything except the unaccountable. He murmured, "When I lay my head in Josephine's lap, and she reads to me in that musical voice of hers, it's worth whatever it costs."

"If you say so."

Napoleon went to bed happy that night. But the next night he had a tantrum when he saw the total figure of Josephine's overdrawn accounts. Hearing about them and seeing them on paper were two different things. In any case, Bonaparte smashed a Louis XIV chair and then wailed over his financial losses. "Josephine, you're driving me to ruin!" he cried.

"In what way have I displeased you now?"

"Everything in your park is prolific," he said grandly. "Everything, except —"

"Go ahead, say it!"

"— except you, Madame."

Josephine wept quietly. She couldn't argue with him about her infertility — what he said was all too true. The costly trips to spas, consultations with mediums, dream trances with the Sorceress — none of these had remedied the nightmare of her insecurity. Now she knew she would not be able to give Napoleon a child.

Nor anyone else.

Ever.

Two days before Christmas in 1803, an ominous cloud hung over the city of Paris. At midday the air was still and cold, and rain began to fall. Lightning fingered the cloud heads.

Then, on Christmas Eve, the storm of the century descended.

"I've seen this before," Josephine said to Hortense. "When I was a small child in Martinique, and I hid my head in my skirt. Outside the thick stone walls of the mill, the wind keened and tore our little world apart."

Hortense pointed out the window of the Tuileries apartment. "Look, Maman, carriages are overturned — carts are being blown away into the river."

"Stand away from the window, *mon ange*."

Hortense took a step backward, but her eyes remained on the terrible storm brewing in the east.

"I wish I could speak to Madame Lenormand," Josephine said as the sky darkened. "She would know what this means."

"Where is she?"

"Bonaparte has her locked up."

Surprised, Hortense turned and gazed into her mother's eyes. "For what reason?"

"He says she's an enemy of the republic. But I think it's because she sees the future, *his* future. Bonaparte doesn't like what she envisions, that's all."

"And what *is* that, Maman?"

"Madame Lenormand had a vision in which he was emperor and I was empress."

"And that made him *angry*?"

Josephine answered uneasily, "I asked her what the price of fulfilling his destiny would be."

"What did she say?"

"She shut her eyes and said, 'Darkness.'"

"Oh." Hortense put her hand to her mouth, and just then a limb torn from a poplar tree came crashing against the side of the Tuileries. Josephine shivered and tried to subdue the gathering storm in her mind. When she closed her eyes, she saw the Sorceress's widely spaced eyes, dark eyebrows, and wild gypsy hair. *The poor woman!* Josephine thought. *All she did was tell the truth. Will I be locked up like that one day? Will I be punished for telling the truth?"*

For the people of Paris, the Christmas Eve storm of 1803 was not something they could shrug off. It seemed a dark portent of sorrows to come. There were many predictions, some apocalyptic — all frightening.

Still, there was magnificence to the events of state. Victory after victory, country after conquered country fell to the machine of war — and all of this was credited to Napoleon.

It appeared that all of Europe lay at his feet. He had returned France to a state of former glory, to the days of ancient monarchy but without the chains of imperial rule. This was a new age ushered in by Napoleon, an age of intelligence in which everyone reveled in the promise of the future.

Yet the machine of war, which lay claim to all of Europe, was unquiet.

And it had chosen the holiest of nights to roar.

That was how the seers saw it — an end was coming. A time of death such as the world had never known.

In 1804, the darkness of Madame Lenormand's vision was greatly offset by pomp and circumstance. The coronation of Napoleon and Josephine, as emperor and empress of the French, distracted the people from the dire events of war. Instead they witnessed the most beautiful ceremony of monarchs that had ever been seen in France.

Cannons and muskets began firing at six o'clock in the evening of December 1, 1804. Paris became a fairy-land of fires and lights, celebrations and fêtes. Braziers burned at every street corner, houses were alight with lamps, and candles burned merrily in every window. The weeks of preparation had kindled public interest and turned it into a furor of fascination. Crowds came to the jeweler's window where the emperor's jeweled crown and diamond-studded sword were on display.

For Josephine the coming affair was a mixed blessing. Finally, her lifetime prophecy was about to be fulfilled. Or was it? Napoleon himself had already spoken of divorce. There were no children from their union, so in his mind, there was no reason to stay married. That is what he said in his darkest moods when he threw all kinds of unreasonable accusations at her.

Poor Josephine lived in a miasma of worry. Her in-laws took advantage of this by torturing her with innuendoes. "There is no crown for you," Madame Letizia said scornfully, and Josephine, full of doubt herself, believed Napoleon's mother. It was certainly possible that, after all this time, Napoleon did not love her enough to keep her and crown her as his queen, his more-than-queen, his empress.

Nor did she know until the very end. Just weeks before the coronation, he rushed into their mirrored bedroom with the news that he had squelched his mother and sisters and brothers by making the announcement public. Josephine was to wear a crown. She was to be crowned. She would be empress after all.

Josephine took the news, as she accepted everything Napoleon brought her, with the sense that it was true, and yet not true. For with Napoleon, anything could happen.

She wore an elaborate robe with the long train that had silver brocade with bees on it — the same bees of Corsican gold that Napoleon was forever drawing in his notebooks. The embroidery in front was all sunlit leaves, with the lower edges fringed and so elegant as not to be believed.

On her bare arms she wore armlets of wrought gold, diamond studded and sparkling. The grace, not to mention strength, that she used to carry this elegant robe of eighty pounds across the inner court of Notre Dame Cathedral took all of her considerable willpower.

The moment the procession reached the throne was when Josephine felt the old Eliama prophecy come true. In that precise moment, the years of waiting were over. The air was sweet with incense, cologne, candles, and the scentless source of her life — destiny.

Closer, closer.

The throne was almost there, almost within reach.

Now a galaxy of stars and bees hovered before the corners of her eyes — her mantle was as unreal as it was beautiful.

Then the eighty-pound robe was suddenly stopped. Josephine froze in her tracks; she couldn't move an inch.

What had happened?

She dared not look behind her; thousands of eyes

were riveted on her every movement. The ceremony of the grand coronation depended on her going forward.

No one knew what was happening. But Josephine thought she divined the danger. The Bonaparte sisters, her worst enemies, had allowed the heavy robe to slip from their hands. The passage to the throne was insurmountable without their help. She stopped, breathed heavily, wondered what to do. Then she heard Napoleon speak sharply. Immediately his three sisters picked up the mantle and the procession continued.

Twenty-four steps remained before attaining the height of the throne, which was set upon a lofty platform. Those twenty-four steps she had to manage all by herself. Summoning all the strength in her body, Josephine inched upward, one stair at a time. The heavy mantle moved by her will alone. Behind her back Josephine heard Napoleon's hateful sisters tittering. *Those devils think I'm ruined. But I will show them how my prophecy shall be fulfilled. More than a queen, more than a queen.*

Slowly, painfully, she ascended the twenty-four stairs to the throne.

Once the coronation ceremony was over, she was greatly relieved. Not only did she receive the resplendent crown, but Napoleon himself planted it lovingly upon her head for all the world to see.

And it was done.

Twenty-nine

Paris, 1806

"He is not a man like other men," Madame Lenormand said in her prison cell. Josephine had finally found her friend, barely alive in the same Carmelite prison where she had spent seven frightful months during the Reign of Terror.

The ancient walls held the screaming souls of ghostly inmates whose names were delicately scripted by sharp fingernails in the crumbling yellow masonry of that hellish place. And now the rats and nits had a fresh supply of flesh to torture.

The old prison remained exactly the same: It was the sepulcher where bones came to lie down and bodies came to die.

Josephine shuddered as she remembered the past.

But the damp eyes of Madame Lenormand gave her heart some cheer. The Sorceress was alive — not well — but at least still alive.

"I don't understand why my husband permits this evil prison to exist." Josephine covered her face with her handkerchief. Behind the lacy cotton, the phantom face of Alexandre crept out and filled her memory. Shivering, she shook off his ghost. "I see only sorrow here. I'm sorry, Madame, but I must go."

Madame Lenormand smiled and clasped Josephine's hand. Her head nodded forward on its thin stalk of neck. The Sorceress peered into the mysterious pattern of whorls. "Your lifeline seems . . . shorter," she whispered.

Josephine tried to pull away, but as always, the Sorceress held on as if the hand belonged to her. "Are you empress yet?" she asked. She brushed a dark wing of raven's hair out of her eyes.

Josephine nodded. "I am empress," she said flatly.

"Ah." The Sorceress's eyes traveled around the cell,

as if seeing there a scene of romantic splendor. "And did the pope crown you?"

"Bonaparte did."

"Ah." She sighed, a faint smile crossing her lips. "And are you happy now?"

Josephine closed her eyes and nodded. Then, just as quickly, she shook her head. A single tear coursed down her left cheek. She breathed deeply, then exhaled.

"You should be happy, *ma chérie*. Your destiny is nearly complete."

"No."

Madame Lenormand's heavy eyelashes fluttered. The dull winter light of the cell shadowed her gaunt face. She was sick, perhaps dying. But her visions kept coming, and she didn't let go of Josephine's imprisoned hand, which she held tighter than ever.

"I see a great fish," said Madame Lenormand, speaking in a trance. "A wicked pike that gobbles up all the smaller fish."

"My husband — is he there?"

254

Madame Lenormand laughed. "He is the great pike, *ma chérie*." She cackled. "He is the ugly fish that swallows all the rest."

"Is that all you see — a big fish?"

Madame Lenormand's smile was a little lopsided. "Now I see a fisherman. His name is Alexander. He sits on a river barge in a white tent. He has many attendants. He is a rich and powerful fisherman. He has but one desire: to catch the pike."

Josephine knew exactly what this meant. Alexander was the Russian czar. There were rumors, she knew, that he was going to betray Napoleon and challenge him with his own army. "What do you see now?" she asked.

Madame Lenormand guffawed. "The pike! The pike! He's been caught by Alexander, the patient fisherman."

Josephine withdrew her hand. She began rubbing it as if it were burned. Tears flooded down her cheeks. She wiped them away with her handkerchief.

"Everything dies in due time," Madame Lenormand said as she concluded her trance.

"Yes, but, my husband — how does *he* die?"

"I have just told you," the Sorceress said. Then, "Did I say something useful?"

"You always say something useful."

The Sorceress added, "A great snow is coming. Did I tell you that?"

"No, you didn't."

Madame Lenormand's gypsy eyes flashed as she groped around in the food basket Josephine had brought her. She broke off a piece of bread and devoured it. "He should never have sent his armies to Moscow in the snow, nor married an Austrian princess."

Josephine, who was pouring the wine into two tin cups, looked up in surprise. "What are you saying? Those things haven't happened."

The Sorceress said, "They will. They will." After a long silence, she spoke again. "You shall die in a mist of flowers."

"Are you in a trance?"

"No, I am eating."

"And my husband?"

"He is not eating, nor is he in a trance."

"I want to know how he will die."

"He suffers because of a ditch."

Josephine eyed her curiously. "You said a river barge."

"That is true: the barge *first*. Then the ditch."

"What ditch?"

"Dashing horsemen will fall into it. Hundreds and hundreds of dashing hussars will bury themselves in a ditch called Waterloo. There will be a terrible hard rain. It will all turn to mud."

"And this ditch, you say . . . the ditch will kill my husband, the pike?"

Madame Lenormand blinked. Her eyes had a wintry glazed look, as if she could see everything — and nothing. "A fish is a fish, a man is a man," she said, lifting her shoulders and letting them fall.

"Which is he, then?"

The Sorceress laughed. She took another bite of bread, another slosh of wine. "He is both," she replied.

"We are going nowhere," Josephine said desperately.

Then Madame Lenormand's eyes locked on Josephine's. "The pike, your husband, the general, he should never have gone so far. He's now got as many people in this prison as Robespierre did."

Josephine gasped. "That's not true. Besides, Bonaparte's not to blame for that."

Madame Lenormand looked fiercely at her. "Who is?"

Josephine shook her head and started to cry. "I fear he's losing his mind — or I'm losing mine, one or the other. Anyway, I will do my best to get you out of here."

Leaving the dank prison of the Carmelite, Josephine returned to Malmaison. As she got out of her carriage, she found herself shaking. She felt unwell. The sight of the prison and the prophetic visions of Madame Lenormand had weakened her. She put white clay on her cheeks. She packed it on, covering every seam, every crack, and she wept as the clay ran in snowy rivers off her face and down into the ditch of her lap.

Thirty

Mainz, France, 1806

It was Talleyrand, smelling lushly of lemons, who told Napoleon he needed to divorce Josephine. Napoleon said nothing. He'd felt this coming for a long time. Still, he bristled at his lank, limping minister telling him what to do.

"It's all for the best," Talleyrand said smoothly.

Napoleon stared at him, maintaining a tense and restive silence. Talleyrand went on, "Your action is not yours alone. It's for the continuance of the empire . . . for France . . . for the future . . . for everyone's benefit."

Napoleon remained silent.

"Josephine is already old," Talleyrand continued. "You must have an heir."

"I *have* one," Bonaparte finally replied, pacing before

a roaring fireplace in the Grand Palace of Mainz, where the family had gone to negotiate a marriage for Eugène with Princess Augusta of Bavaria.

"I was referring to a legitimate heir."

Napoleon snorted, giving his minister a sharp glance. Talleyrand shrugged it off and limped back from the mammoth fireplace. "Who burns winter wood in the spring?" he questioned, shaking his head.

"I like it warm," Napoleon said.

"You like it *hot*. Do you not perceive the difference?"

"I *perceive*," said Napoleon, "a one-legged minister to whom I must unfortunately cleave like a vine while at the same time I must break off with my beloved wife of fourteen years. Can *you* perceive a difference?"

Talleyrand dabbed at his perspiring forehead with a brocaded handkerchief, and sighed plaintively.

"You're losing your precious hair, my witty minister," Bonaparte noted with a thin-lipped grin.

"You are losing an *heir* if you don't do as I say."

Napoleon turned his back on Talleyrand and

examined the orange serpents of flames that filled the cavernous fireplace of the Grand Palace's most regal guest chamber.

"Very well," he said at last. His chin was cupped in his hand, his back was still turned to Talleyrand, and he was slightly hunched over, staring at the lapping firelight. "I will do what you . . . want."

Talleyrand's face brightened. "No, sire, what the empire —"

"Yes, sire, no, sire, what the empire, sire," Napoleon mimicked in a raspy voice. Then, turning from the bonfire, he faced Talleyrand and closed the small distance between them.

"So I will therefore do what my idiot mother, my pinhead brother, my fathead brother, and my three stone-hearted sisters desire. You see, Talleyrand, it's not enough that I've given them *kingdoms*, my siblings now want me to marry a royal like each of them has done. Now, it's done, and we can be done with it. I'll banish Josephine to Malmaison, and she'll be happier there among her zebras than she is here with these hyenas of Bavaria."

Chastened, Talleyrand said nothing.

In the end it wasn't Talleyrand who broke the news of the divorce to Josephine. He bowed out of that duty, as well as Hortense and Eugène. Joseph Fouché, the minister of police, offered his services. He didn't mind telling her at all, he said. What was this? Just another onerous duty he had to perform in the service of his city, his country.

Josephine, when she saw Fouché enter the foyer at Malmaison, could read his face even before he spoke. She knew exactly what he was going to say before he said it.

It was a warm July day. As usual, Josephine's hands had been deep in the dark earth that morning, planting and pruning, and pinching the caterpillars that clustered on her oleanders. These were just a few of her early morning duties. She hated killing caterpillars, but someone had to — and now she saw the heavy, caterpillarlike chin whiskers of Fouché, and she read his mind like she could read a plant that needs water.

He came on, heavy-footed, lumbering, and furry.

Still, when he delivered his message, Josephine smiled and leaned against a doorjamb. Then she fainted. Fouché rushed to catch her. She awoke in his arms, saw his hairy face, and screamed. "It's all right, Madame, I have you now," Fouché said, trying to quiet her. The deed had been done. Josephine had been informed.

At the Tuileries, some days later, Napoleon begged her forgiveness. "I was planning to tell you myself. But then Hortense seemed a much better choice. She refused. So then I asked Eugène if he'd do it; he said no, he couldn't bear to. That left me. I still couldn't do it. I'm weak, I admit it — so I asked Fouché. He said yes."

"Why Fouché, of all people?"

Napoleon grimaced. "He's good at sordid details."

Josephine smiled painfully. "He was awful."

"Won't you always read to me?"

Josephine, her eyes brimming with tears that didn't

fall, whispered, "How can you ask me such a thing after what you've done?"

"Because I still love you." His eyes, too, were tearful when he said this.

"Then why are you leaving me?" she asked.

"I've already explained that to you."

They were talking in the privacy of their blue canopied bed, the one she'd designed for him. It was very late, and quite hot. As usual, Napoleon had lighted a fire, which burned warmly as they conversed.

"Must you always imagine you are in camp, Bonaparte?"

"Yes, with my daughters, the cannons," he mused, his long-tailed nightcap fallen across his face.

"With the crying of the wounded is more like it."

Napoleon pressed his lips together. His eyes burned brightly in the fire's glow.

Josephine looked sadly at her husband and shook her head. "I love you," she said sighing. "I shall always love you."

"You're still — and always — my guiding star, Josephine, my Josephine."

In the months that followed the divorce, which was mercifully swift, Josephine toiled in the greenhouse at Malmaison. There, among her precious plants and exotic flowers, she lived in the warm pathos of memory, the delicate province of dream.

Often — at least once a day — she recalled the coronation, her brief moment of pure glory, and the apotheosis of her entire life.

All day long, now, she pinched buds, scattered seeds, watered the soil, and remembered. . . .

How could she forget Bonaparte with his imperial purple robe lined in ermine, and his snow-white heron-plumed hat? It was something to see, that was.

And what about her own satin gown, afire with diamonds, that was outdone only by her own splendid, twenty-foot robe?

And Josephine could never forget the faces of her

detractors, the Bonaparte sisters, when Napoleon placed the crown upon her head. They seemed to shrink. She saw them wither in that gilded moment.

But now even that triumph seemed far away and unimportant.

What was she?

No more an empress, much less than a queen.

Josephine was only a mistress of memory in a vast windowed house of flowers on an estate called Malmaison, which Marie-Louise, Napoleon's new wife, wanted to take away from her.

At Malmaison, Josephine lived in the spirit more than the flesh, immersing herself in her botanical work and her research into lost time. As the ice cracked and crunched along the banks of the Seine, she was breathing the warm, tropical air of her childhood.

Dignitaries came and went. Alexander I, czar of Russia, King Frederick William III of Prussia, and all the lesser princes of Europe paid her homage and looked benevolently at her impassioned plantings — jasmine from La Pagerie in Martinique, poppies from the Nile in Egypt that had been ferried all the way home in Bonaparte's boots. Josephine's famous orchids were beloved by all who chanced to view them, for they seemed to honor a time of fading glory. Yet, though Josephine was seen as an orchid angel hovering over her gentle blossoms, in her heart she was deeply wounded.

"I cannot overcome the fearful sadness that has seized me," she said one day to a friend of Hortense's. "I do all I can to hide my cares from my children, but I suffer only the more." She confessed, "You will see that Napoleon's misfortune will cause my death. My heart is broken — it will not be healed."

In the fields of battle, Napoleon's misfortune became more and more obvious. His losses multiplied, and his victories were blighted by more losses. Married to Marie-Louise, the nineteen-year-old archduchess of Austria, he had exactly what Talleyrand told him he needed — what he'd always desired: a son, an heir who was called the king of Rome. But Bonaparte's eyes were not on his apocryphal child. His eyes were fixed on empires he yet wished to conquer — Russia, England, Spain, and America.

All the while, Josephine dug deeper than ever into the mysterious fortunes of her flowers. She dined with them and dressed like them. Traveling outside of Malmaison, she wore the colors of evening blossoms — pastel muslins that concealed her age and her waist.

Amidst many guests, she was always alone. She wept at any time of day, for any reason at all. She had constant headaches. Once in a great while, she was visited by Napoleon, who was courteous and restrained. Nonetheless, he was still her general. She was still his star.

Deep down, however, Napoleon knew that his star had abandoned him because he had abandoned it, or rather her. In battle he looked old and fatigued. He needed help mounting his horse. His stomach troubled him. His back ached. When he returned from Russia, his Grand Army was all but gone. Three-quarters of a million troops had crossed the Nieman River near Kovno in Poland, and only a few thousand half-frozen soldiers had returned alive. After that, Bonaparte drafted children to fight for France. And though those who fought for the empire were young, the empire had, in only fifteen years, grown irretrievably old.

For Josephine, the best was over, the worst still to come. Yet it was all just as Madame Lenormand had predicted. The great pike had swallowed the world and vomited it up. Even gold-domed Moscow had gone down his gullet. But now, the pike was caught, his time on earth was nearly over, and Josephine dreamed no longer of Eliama under the moon of Martinique. Josephine had no regrets. As she said, "I married more than a king, and I have lost more than an empire."

Thirty-one

Malmaison, Elba, & St. Helena, 1814~1821

In 1812, Napoleon continued to wage war — mostly without success. Finally, he was captured and sentenced by the English to permanent exile on the island of Elba. There on the temperate Mediterranean isle not far from Corsica where he was born, Napoleon kept his court and even his sense of humor. Often, he thought of Josephine. His last letter to her came from Elba:

> *I shall substitute the pen for the sword. The narrative . . . will be surprising; people have seen me only in profile, and I shall show myself full face. They have betrayed me, yes, all of them. I accept only our dear Eugène, so worthy of you and of me. May he be happy*

under a king who can appreciate the instincts of nature
and honor! Adieu, my dear Josephine. Resign yourself,
as I am doing, and never lose the memory of one who
has never forgotten you, and never will.

N. B.

In March 1815, Napoleon accomplished his wish by secretly foiling his English enemies and effecting a daring escape on the brigantine *Inconstant*. Once back on French soil he gathered an army of one thousand men, forty horses, and two cannons. Marching to Paris as a conquering hero, Napoleon called together more men — and children — and fought his final battle in the fields of Belgium. By then his tiny force had grown into an army of twenty thousand. However, it was there at Waterloo where, as Madame Lenormand had predicted, an unseen ditch swallowed up his best cavalry, then his infantry, and then his hopes. Bad weather and the lack of reserves stopped him in the end. Mired in mud, he could do nothing, and for the first time in their history, Napoleon's sodden soldiers retreated on the run. A few thousand more infantry and Napoleon might have trumped the English, as he himself knew. But it did not happen that way. After Waterloo Napoleon was exiled to the barren British island of St. Helena, off the west coast of Africa. There he wrote his memoirs and lived on for six more years.

Josephine remained at Malmaison "in a mist of flowers." One evening, while sitting under a bower of purple magnolias, she remembered one perfect summer evening, perhaps the happiest of her life with Napoleon. Then he was well and full of fun. That was how she liked to remember him now, full of playful tricks . . . so . . . Bonaparte.

She and her friends had been wandering about in the summer air, watching the swallows dive. She had a little cup full of bluets she'd just picked. Bonaparte came up behind her. He had a handful of dirt, and he drowned the bluets in it.

"Bonaparte, how could you?" Josephine looked at him in bewilderment.

He laughed, but when he saw her tears, he rushed off and picked a fresh bouquet for her. Lovingly he put more bluets into her cup.

Bonaparte, you devil, you angel. I cannot write the way you can. I cannot will myself to the world as you will. Let someone else tell my tale, if they should wish to. I am done with everything but memory. In that I am still more than a queen.

One night, Josephine brought forth another recollection — the time she'd imprisoned him. It was just after the coronation, and Bonaparte had said, "Let's play capture the flag."

"There's barely enough light," she had told him. "You'll run into something and hurt yourself."

But Bonaparte cared nothing for injuries — neither his own nor others'. Twenty torches were lighted and carried about in the dark by valets, and the Malmaison night sparked as if lighted up by human fireflies.

Josephine, nimble and fast, slipped away whenever

Bonaparte tried to capture her. But he — in his loose white shirt — was an easy target for her. She caught him quickly, and pinned him to the grass. "You're my prisoner now," she said with a grin.

"I — a *prisoner?*" he said in disgust.

"Say you surrender," she cried, holding him as tightly as she could. The torches in the field came nearer and nearer.

Napoleon struggled, but Josephine managed to keep him down. The moon hung over the poplar trees.

"I will *never* surrender," he said with a groan.

"Not even to me?" she asked.

At once his face softened. "I gave in to you long ago," he said.

And they kissed as the firefly torches formed a fairy ring all around them.

That perfect summer night was on her mind in May 1814, when, lying on her deathbed, Josephine closed her eyes for the last time and spoke one last word: "Bonaparte."

Napoleon wasted away exactly as the English intended. Fed arsenic poison in his food and wine, his skin waxed yellow in color. He weakened and did not know why. Nor was it any comfort to him knowing that the old royalist family of France had returned to power with the installation of King Louis XVIII. A short time before his death, some six years after Josephine died, Napoleon told his secretary, Comte Joseph Las Cases, "I ought not to have allowed myself to be separated from Josephine. That was my downfall." Separate or apart, Napoleon and Josephine both died as they had lived — bound to each other, prisoners of the heart.

Chronology

JUNE 23, 1763.	Marie-Josèphe Rose Tascher de La Pagerie born in Martinique, French West Indies.
AUGUST 15, 1769.	Nabuleone Buonoparte born in Ajaccio, Corsica.
MAY 13, 1770.	Napoleon enters École Militaire at Brienne, France.
OCTOBER 12, 1779.	Rose arrives in France.
DECEMBER 13, 1779.	Rose marries Alexandre de Beauharnais.
SEPTEMBER 3, 1781.	Eugène Beauharnais is born.
APRIL 10, 1783.	Hortense Beauharnais is born.
MARCH 5, 1785.	The separation of Rose and Alexandre is legalized.
JUNE 20, 1791.	Alexandre Beauharnais is elected president of the National Assembly.
JANUARY 21, 1793.	King Louis XVI is beheaded.
OCTOBER 16, 1793.	Queen Marie-Antoinette is beheaded.
FEBRUARY 1794.	Napoleon is appointed commander of artillery in Italy.

MARCH 2, 1794.	Alexandre Beauharnais is arrested and imprisoned at Les Carmes.
APRIL 20, 1794.	Rose is arrested and imprisoned at Les Carmes.
JULY 23, 1794.	Alexandre Beauharnais is beheaded.
JULY 28, 1794.	Maximilien Robespierre is beheaded.
AUGUST 6, 1794.	Rose is released from prison.
SEPTEMBER 1795.	Rose meets Napoleon and their relationship begins.
MARCH 9, 1796.	Rose changes her name to Josephine to please Napoleon. Josephine and Napoleon marry in a civil ceremony in Paris.
MARCH 11, 1796.	Napoleon is appointed commander in chief of the Army of Italy.
OCTOBER 17, 1797.	Napoleon is appointed commander of forces for the invasion of England.
MAY 19, 1798.	Napoleon sets sail for Egypt.
APRIL 21, 1799.	Josephine buys Malmaison.
OCTOBER 14, 1799.	Napoleon returns to France.
NOVEMBER 9/10, 1800.	Napoleon establishes himself first consul.
FEBRUARY 19, 1800.	Josephine and Napoleon move to the Tuileries.

JUNE 14, 1800.	Napoleon defeats Austria at the Battle of Marengo.
DECEMBER 24, 1800.	Napoleon escapes assassination attempt in Paris.
AUGUST 2, 1802.	Napoleon is appointed first consul for life.
MARCH 21, 1804.	Napoleon creates the Civil Code, also known as the Code Napoleon.
DECEMBER 2, 1804.	Napoleon and Josephine are crowned emperor and empress of the French.
1805–1809.	Napoleon's military superiority on land is established in a series of decisive European battles. On July 7, 1807, Napoleon signs Treaty of Tilsit with Czar Alexander I and Frederick William III of Prussia.
DECEMBER 15, 1809.	Napoleon and Josephine are divorced.
MARCH 1809–APRIL 1814.	Josephine retires to Château de Navarre at Evereaux and Malmaison.
APRIL 2, 1810.	Napoleon marries Marie-Louise, archduchess of Austria.
MARCH 20, 1811.	Napoleon's son, Napoleon Francis, is born.
JUNE 24, 1812–DECEMBER 5, 1812.	Napoleon successfully enters Moscow but is defeated by the Russian winter.

MAY 2, 1813– OCTOBER 19, 1813.	Napoleon defeats Prussians and Russians at Lutzen, but is later defeated at the Battle of Leipzig.
APRIL 11, 1814.	Napoleon abdicates at Fontainebleau, France.
APRIL 20, 1814.	Napoleon is exiled to Elba, in Italy.
MAY 3, 1814.	King Louis XVIII returns to France.
MAY 29, 1814.	Josephine dies at Malmaison.
FEBRUARY 26, 1815.	Napoleon escapes from Elba.
MARCH 26, 1815.	Napoleon returns to Paris as emperor.
JUNE 18, 1815.	Napoleon abdicates for the second time.
JULY 8, 1815.	Louis XVIII returns to the Tuileries.
AUGUST 7, 1815.	Napoleon departs for exile in St. Helena, off the west coast of Africa.
MAY 5, 1821.	Napoleon dies in St. Helena.

Bibliography

ABRANTES, DUCHESS. *At the Court of Napoleon: Memoirs of the Duchess d'Abrantes*. New York: Doubleday, 1989.

CHANDLER, DAVID. *The Illustrated Napoleon*. New York: Henry Holt, 1990.

CORZINE, PHYLLIS. *The French Revolution*. San Diego: Lucent Books, 1995.

DeLORME, ELEANOR. *Josephine: Napoleon's Incomparable Empress*. New York: Harry Abrams Inc., 2002.

DUMAS, ALEXANDRE. *The Count of Monte Cristo*. New York: Modern Library, 1996.

————. *The Three Musketeers*. Laurel, NY: Lightyear Press, 1976.

ERICKSON, CAROLLY. *Josephine: A Life of an Empress*. New York: St. Martin's Press, 1998.

FERMOR, PATRICK. *The Traveller's Tree: A Journey Through the Caribbean Islands*. New York: Harper and Brothers, 1950.

GULLAND, SANDRA. *The Many Lives and Secret Sorrows of Josephine B.* New York: Scribner, 1995.

————. *Tales of Passion, Tales of Woe*. New York: Scribner, 1998.

————. *The Last Great Dance on Earth*. New York: Scribner, 2000.

HIBBERT, CHRISTOPHER. *Versailles*. New York, Newsweek Books, 1972.

————. *Napoleon: His Wives and Women*. New York: W. W. Norton, 2002.

JOHNSON & HAYTHORNWAITHE. *In the Words of Napoleon*. Harrisburg, PA: Stackpole Books, 2002.

KIRCHBERGER, JOE. *The French Revolution and Napoleon: An Eyewitness History*. New York: Facts on File, 1989.

LENORMAND, MADAME. *The Secret and Historical Memoirs of the Empress Josephine: Vol. I & II*. London: H. S. Nichols, 1865.

LEVER, EVELINE. *Marie Antoinette.* New York: Farrar, Strauss & Giroux, 2000.

MARRIN, ALBERT. *Napoleon and the Napoleonic Wars.* New York: Viking, 1991.

McLYNN, FRANK. *Napoleon.* New York: Arcade Publishing, 1997.

MOSSIKER, FRANCES. *Napoleon and Josephine: The Biography of a Marriage.* New York: Simon and Schuster, 1964.

————. *More Than a Queen.* New York: Knopf, 1971.

MUHLBACH, L. *The Empress Josephine: An Historical Sketch of the Days of Napoleon.* New York: D. Appleton, Co., 1897.

THOMPSON. J. M. *Napoleon Bonaparte.* England: Sutton, 2001.